Praise for Nicole Austin's *Tamara's Spirit*

"All signs point to Corralled being a long running... innovative series."

~*Just Erotic Romance Reviews*

"I found myself carried away and couldn't put it down."

~ *Joyfully Reviewed*

"I was thrilled to read the epilogue and find out that our 'cowboy' Jesse is next up in this series to receive his own story. Hurry up Ms. Austin, I can hardly wait for the next one to be published!"

~ *The Romance Studio*

"Nicole Austin has yet again amazed me with her true sensuality and romantic heart, her talent is truly phenomenal. Ms. Austin pulls you into this story so you will feel the amazing depth of their spiritual bond. Come visit the Shooting Star Ranch and read for yourself. I promise you won't be disappointed."

~ *Sensual Reads*

Tamara's Spirit

Book Two of the Corralled Series

Nicole Austin

A Samhain Publishing, Ltd. publication.

Samhain Publishing, Ltd.
512 Forest Lake Drive
Warner Robins, GA 31093
www.samhainpublishing.com

Tamara's Spirit
Copyright © 2006 by Nicole Austin
Print ISBN: 1-59998-734-1
Digital ISBN: 1-59998-451-2

Editing by Angela James
Cover by Anne Cain

First Samhain Publishing, Ltd. electronic publication: April 2007
First Samhain Publishing, Ltd. print publication: February 2008

Dedication

To NJ Walters. Thanks for helping me find a name for Tamara's bookstore. Your input, as well as your friendship, is greatly appreciated.

To my family. As always, thank you for the support and encouragement.

Prologue

"What's eating you?"

Well, certainly not any of my cowboys, as they should be.

Stephanie's question was a good one, but one Tamara wasn't about to answer with any real honesty. Instead, she mumbled something noncommittal and was glad when Cord's sister took the hint and left her alone.

Being forced to endure so much beauty, bliss and wedding day happiness made her want to puke. She stood at the reception and kept glancing outside, wondering how much she had to suffer through. How long she should stay before making her escape? She needed to get the hell outta there.

The majestic mountains, ever present guardians of all that lay below, wore an incandescent patina of amber, garnet and amethyst. Jagged spikes of aged gray rock soared upward into the vast, endless blue Montana sky. Lush, emerald green grasses covered the valley. It had been a picture perfect day for the ceremony, and was turning into a gorgeous night.

Without question, the Shooting Star ranch lands held regal beauty. And everyone who had gathered around the blissful couple fit together with both the land and each other, like pieces of a puzzle forming a complete picture.

Everyone excluding Tamara. They were all blind to the reality she was like one of those stray puzzle pieces which never seemed to fit in anywhere, no matter how you struggled to make it conform to the mold. The picture was complete without it being there, and when you tried to force it to fit, you created an obvious flaw within the beautiful design. For some reason, she was the only one who saw this apparent truth.

Taking a deep, fortifying breath, she moved farther into the tent where the reception was already in progress and stood off to the side taking everything in.

Before the festivities, Savannah had sat all of them down and with calm, quiet assurance explained how she thought of them like family. Her goal was to keep them all together. She then handed sealed envelopes to each of the cowboys, the bookkeeper and Tamara. Inside each packet was a deed for ten acres of Shooting Star ranch lands.

What the heck Van thought Tamara was supposed to do with ten acres of ranch land was beyond her comprehension. The crazy woman said they should each build a house, start a family. Tamara had almost choked and spewed her coffee everywhere at the suggestion.

Speak of the devil, Savannah wandered over to her side. Her friend looked gorgeous in her white gown, natural. Van belonged here. In fact, she was in her element. "Penny for your thoughts."

Watching Cord courting Savannah over the past few months had ignited a fathomless hunger Tamara had managed to keep subjugated within the deepest recesses of her soul. It had created an insatiable yearning for some nameless but vital element which had long been missing for years, leaving her incomplete. While the cowboys were able to ease her burning sexual ache, they were unable to fill the void. Yet focusing on sex with her boys was much more pleasant than dwelling on an anonymous ache she had no hope of fulfilling.

Of course, she didn't dare bring up her relationship with the cowboys now. It was bad enough everyone knew about their group sex activities after Savannah had caught the five of them in the act.

"They're not worth that much." She knew the reply was flippant, but was running out of forced good humor. "My mind is just wandering a bit today and I'm a bit antsy." Truth of the matter, Tamara was totally out of sorts.

In retrospect, moving to the ranch had not been such a good idea. Daily exposure to the loving couples in residence had begun to erode her sanity and increased the ache. If only she could put a name to the elusive missing facet, she'd be able to embark on a search.

Or maybe not. Even if she did name *it*, capture *it*—was she worthy enough to keep *it*? Maybe she wasn't supposed to have *it*, even if she did know what *it* was. Some things were best left alone.

Watching her friends celebrate the marriage and happiness over the gift of the land was torture. They were all in such high spirits.

"You can talk to me about anything, Tam." Van's expression was encouraging, but there was no way Tamara would bring her friend's spirits down on her special day.

Oh, how she hated weddings, no matter how elegant or tastefully conducted. They made her think too much. While Cord and Savannah Black's wedding had been divine, it still sucked to have to attend.

A single tear had escaped Tamara's bright, jade green eye as the joyous couple had rode off toward the mountains before everyone made their way to the reception. Watching them ride away together stirred emotions she did not want to deal with. Not in this century.

"Come on. Tell me what's wrong." Savannah's persistence wore on her, but there was no way she'd speak this particular internal soundtrack out loud.

Tamara really needed to get out of there before her bad mood darkened Van's happy day, but it was too soon to leave...wasn't it?

The festivities at the reception were abject torture, but they'd barely gotten underway. She would have to suffer in silence through the obtuse, jubilant nuptial rites yet to take place. How laughable the only single women fighting over the bouquet would be her, an eight year old girl, and Stephanie. The implied meaning of catching the flowers made her shudder with revulsion.

As expected, the available men would then fight over the garter flung over Cord's shoulder. Then the real absurdity would begin as the lucky winner was bestowed with the dubious honor of sliding his prize as far up the lady's leg as she allowed.

Tamara breathed a heavy sigh. "You know I hate this kind of stuff, Van."

While the dancing was enjoyable, in the end it would leave her needing to be fucked, and all the drinking would render the cowboys useless to slake her thirst. Once again she'd be left aching.

Savannah enveloped her into a warm hug. "Aw, hon, I'm sorry. Get out of here if you need to. I'll try not to worry about you sulking the night away alone in your cabin."

Oh great, rub it in and hit me with a major guilt trip why don't ya, pal.

"One day soon a man will come along who can see past the Barney badass attitude to the beautiful soul you struggle so hard to hide."

Tamara had to wonder if Van was making a general statement or if her friend had actually had a vision of the future, but decided she wasn't real anxious to know which it was. Tamara pointed across the tent at Cord, who watched them closely. "Your husband is waiting for you to dance with him."

Her friend's smile brightened when she looked over at the big cowboy. Savannah patted Tamara's forearm, then scurried off to Cord's side. *Whew.* At least Van had been easy to distract.

She didn't understand why Van went and married Cord. They had a great thing going, and marriage would probably only screw it up. Hell, her beautiful friend could get any man she wanted. Why did she want to restrict herself to just one? Tamara frowned, unable to imagine tying herself to one man when there were so many waiting for her attentions.

While not on the same level as gorgeous, curvy Van, Tamara still thought she looked pretty good. And there was never any shortage of men available for her to sleep with. Lots of men liked small women and, in her estimation, at five-five she wasn't too short, she was perfect. It was all the huge men around the ranch making her feel tiny. Okay, so maybe she'd like her not-quite-B-cup breasts to be a little larger, but overall she felt good about her looks.

She'd learned long ago not to get attached to any man. The typical life cycle of her relationships was about four months before the guy began to cling. In most cases she was long gone before then, the one exception being the hunky Shooting Star cowboys. Zeke, Jesse, Brock and Riley had shared her for several months now with no annoying signs of possessiveness. *Yeehaw!*

Although the sex was fabulous, it was starting to become boring, taking more and more for her to reach satisfaction.

Much like a drug addict, each time requiring more to achieve their high. The same was true for Tamara. Each sexual encounter took a bit more in order for her to get off.

As if he'd sensed she was thinking about him, Zeke ambled over, grabbed her arm and swung her around. "Dance with me, beautiful."

The words weren't slurred too badly, and he still seemed to have a good deal of coordination left, but she had no desire to hit the makeshift dance floor.

"No thanks, cowboy. Why don't you go ask the sister of the groom? She looks ready to boogie." The bitch in question was currently batting her eyelashes at Riley. Tamara wasn't sure she liked Steph paying attention to *her* cowboys. Especially since the guys were taking notice. However, using Steph to distract Zeke worked in her favor now.

Zeke smiled, tipped his hat, and sauntered off toward where Stephanie stood, tapping her foot and swaying in time to the music.

Maybe what I need is a drastic change.

Leave everything behind and set out on an adventure. She'd always wanted to travel, but wandering the world alone? Somehow she knew the experience would leave her feeling even more restless and unsettled. Hell, she hated to be alone anyway. There was nothing worse than quiet solitude. It's when all of her demons came out to play.

She shook her head. Damn, what was she thinking? She couldn't leave Savannah anyway. Her friend would need her support during neighboring rancher Wyatt Bodine's trial. Cord would be supportive, but she'd want Tamara by her side to face the vile man who'd terrorized both Savannah and Mandy Morton, the ranch bookkeeper's young daughter.

Soon her friend would be wrapped up with the growing ranch, her new husband, and the birth of her baby, though. Tamara wouldn't be missed anymore when that happened. Then it would be glaringly apparent she didn't belong on the ranch and there would be nothing to keep her from drifting away.

Right now she needed to get through the wedding frippery. She'd be so relieved when the happy affair was over. Her cheeks were sore from efforts to maintain a counterfeit smile. Would the fabricated cheer be obvious in the pictures? Did it even matter? Most likely no one would even notice if she left the party early. Van had already given the okay for her to get out of there.

"What's eating you?" Brock asked. The way too serious cowboy appeared at her side, his lips thinned with concern beneath the sable mustache she loved to feel caress her tender skin.

"Nothing. Can't you tell how fandamntastic I'm feeling?" Was it so obvious she was completely uncomfortable?

"You look great, babe."

"Are you trying to be obtuse, Brock? I guess I should make it crystal clear. I have PMS and a handgun in my clutch," she lied. "If I were you, I'd stay far away."

He gave her a startled look and made a quick getaway to the bar. Smart man!

A black cloud of depression descended on her. Maybe she needed medication. Those commercials with the sad face which ended up bounding after a butterfly always made her wonder. All the symptoms they listed fit. Feeling sad, anxious, restless, having no interest in activities. At times she felt intense urges to flee, felt trapped, heart pounding, palms clammy, nauseous...

She shook off her mental wanderings. No, drugs were not the answer. No feel-good medication would wash away her restless needs and jaded senses.

Riley and Jesse decided on a tag team effort in approaching her. In her peripheral vision, Tamara caught sight of the two fools attempting to sneak up on her. What was with these guys? Why didn't they get the obvious? She didn't want company. In fact, she was perfectly happy with her misery as a companion.

"Don't even think about it, boys!" The words were spoken in a deep, menacing tone which sent the two men scurrying off in different directions.

The material of the large white tent, erected to contain the reception, began to waver in the gentle breeze, giving the impression it was closing in on her. Tamara's chest tightened in apprehension, and she decided now was the time to make her escape.

She stepped out into the balmy evening and took in a deep lungful of crisp, clean air. "Ah, much better."

Torches provided an amber glow to light the way through the dark night. The spiked heels she wore sunk into rich earth as she moved toward her cabin.

Making her way over the rustic terrain required all her attention when the meager light ended, leaving her in the inky blackness of a moonless night. She moved with focused determination and haste while closely watching where she trod, head down. If she stepped in some steaming pile of horse shit with these expensive shoes on...

When she turned the corner of the main house, she walked right into a large object, driving much needed oxygen from her lungs with a whoosh. She lifted her hands and pressed her open palms against the obstacle, giving a firm shove. The solid mass never budged.

"Whoa. Hello there, gorgeous. Are you all right?"

If he hadn't already knocked the air from her lungs, the stranger's sexy drawl would have taken her breath away. She looked up into compelling eyes, which drove all coherent thought from her mind.

Oh God, what was wrong with her? She'd always had the ability to come back with some cocky crack. For some reason, nothing came to mind other than how mysterious and dangerous the big man looked in the low light cast from the porch lamp. His dark appearance gave her the impression of a rakish bad boy, but there was also something inherent in his presence that created a calming affect.

Warm hands held her hips in a firm grip. It was a good thing too, because her legs felt rubbery and ready to give out. Her nostrils flared, drinking in his masculine scent. She smelled leather, sun-warmed flesh and hot man. Tamara swayed, feeling dizzy.

"I've gotcha," the stranger declared.

The world whirled around and dipped in a wild motion. Cold chills raised goose bumps on her arms. Damn it, she wasn't the kind of frail woman prone to fainting. What the hell was wrong with her? It wasn't like she'd been drinking at the reception.

When things settled again, she found herself planted tight and secure against a wide torso. Muscular arms held her snug as steel bands around her back and under her legs. She threw her arms around the thick column of his neck, clinging to him. Then the big stranger carried her to the porch steps, only instead of putting her down as she expected, he sat with her held captive on his lap.

It would be heaven to sink into his chest, absorbing his abundant warmth. She tilted her head and looked into those penetrating black eyes. Raven blue-black hair gleamed around his shoulders in the soft light. His dark skin held the deep cinnamon tones of Native American heritage.

Well, holy shit! She'd been captured by an Indian. Where the hell were her cowboys when she needed to be rescued? Talk about ironic. Scrambling to free herself from his grasp, Tamara pushed against his substantial chest again with little effect on the big man.

"Let go."

He ignored her demand and struggles. When she huffed in frustration her captor finally spoke. "Easy now, princess. I won't hurt you."

"Wh–Who are you? What are you doing skulking around in the dark?" He might be some crazed axe murderer for all she knew. It was always the cute ones, wasn't it?

His smile was a luminous flash of white teeth tugging at her heart, irregardless of whatever type of man he may be. She could get lost merely drinking in his captivating features. And oh, how she wanted to feel his silky ebony hair slip between her fingers. Heat flooded her pussy at the thought of fisting her hands in the shoulder length strands and holding him captive between her wide spread legs.

Luscious, plump lips called out for her tongue to explore their texture and shape. His firm jaw looked as if it were chiseled from granite. Massive shoulders led to his solid, muscular chest. Without realizing, she flexed her fingers, basking in the pure masculine vitality and power within her grasp.

"Dakota Blackhawk, at your service. I was hired last week by Mister Black. He told me I was free to start moving in whenever I was ready."

Tamara stared at him, stunned. No one had told her a new guy had been hired. She was so out of the loop, but maybe she wouldn't leave the ranch after all. Things would become quite interesting with Dakota working and living on the Shooting Star. And did she really want the cowboys coming to the rescue?

Maybe not.

She wondered for a moment if he heard the racing of her heart, which was beating triple time. Oh the delicious adventures she'd have exploring the yummy man who still held her. The feel of his thumb stroking over the pulse point in her wrist had her pussy lips drenched with hot cream. The sweet pressure and heat of his very large, erect cock against her hip were divine. And his firm legs beneath her bottom...yum.

"What's your name, princess? Do you live here?"

"I...um." Hell, her mind was so muddled she wasn't even able to remember her name. "Tamara. Tamara Dobbs. Yes, I live on the ranch with my friends. We all live here. I'm the only one who doesn't work here though."

Oh, God. She was rambling on like a total idiot. The way he was looking at her, and his sexy voice, took the quick wit she prided herself on and sent it packing. If only talking to him and sitting on his lap made her feel like this, what would it be like to have him in her bed? Mmm...or in her Jeep, or the back aisle of the bookstore, or at the lake. The delightful possibilities were endless.

Yes, ranch life just became a great deal more interesting since running into Dakota Blackhawk.

CR80

He walked along the moonlit path, his mind was wrapped up in work. He was anxious to get started first thing in the morning, and was busy creating a mental to-do list.

Dakota caught a brief glimpse of the radiant little princess a mere second before she crashed into him, scattering his thoughts to the wind. One look into her green eyes, sparkling in the low light, and a soul-deep feeling of connection formed inside him.

"Whoa. Hello there, gorgeous. Are you all right?"

Intense awareness flowed through Dakota, making him wonder if she could be the woman he'd longed to find. His other half, a spirit mate.

She looked at him with such an open, awed expression. He read a range of emotions passing over those delicate features— hope, longing, insecurity, and distance.

Then the spirited sprite pulled her emotions under control and tried to shove him away. Dakota smiled with satisfaction. She had spunk, determination and a strong backbone. He liked that. The feisty woman would make life interesting. Sensing the struggle ahead, he began the careful planning of his next steps.

Wow! Life sure kept getting better.

He got the impression for a few moments he'd seen a side of the small woman not often revealed, if ever even hinted at. Without the slightest hesitation, he gathered her wavering form into his arms, his heart clenching at the glimpse of vulnerability crossing her exotic features. She must feel the strong connection too.

He offered up a silent prayer of thanks to the Great Spirit for this gift, vowing to cherish every moment.

"I've gotcha." And was it ever wonderful. He held her with care, unwilling to relinquish the physical contact when they reached the porch steps. Holding her in his arms felt right, further convincing Dakota she was his true mate. Finding her here at the ranch was a welcome surprise.

The small, dark-haired sprite pulled her intense sexuality around herself like a shield. Smoldering jade eyes looked up at him, giving him a provocative glance from under long, thick lashes. Shiny mahogany tresses fell in gentle waves to bare shoulders. The change in her happened so fast Dakota felt like he should have whiplash as a result. From vulnerable sprite one instant, to skilled seductress the next.

The pale peach silken dress she wore fit every delicate curve of her slender body. A thin halter strap held up the bodice, which was slit down the center past her navel where a delicate silver ring hung. The entire back of the garment was open, dipping dangerously low over the small of her back. At the point of contact where her bare skin touched his arm, he felt a blistering heat. Blatant, innate sexuality radiated from every fiber of her being.

Dakota sensed she would put up a fierce fight, but he had no doubt he would win her heart and soul. This was not a woman who would give her love without a great deal of effort, but he felt up to the challenge. His ancestors were spiritual healers, and helping his spirit mate mend her heart path was his one true destiny.

Tamara questioned who he was, and what he was doing roaming around the darkened ranch. She morphed into a sexy vixen in moments, making his head spin.

"Mmm, and what exactly were you hired for, stud?" she purred, pulling Dakota from his thoughts. Her voice took on a husky, self-assured tone, sending frissons of heat echoing through his veins. He imagined her speaking dark, seductive words in that sexy tone against his ear as they made love.

"I'm a horse trainer. I'll be working on the breeding and training program with Savannah."

Dakota smiled as Tamara stood, gathered her dress high up on her thighs, then straddled his lap. In a blatant, sexual move, she began rubbing her hot pussy against his hard cock. It wouldn't take much to give her what she was asking for. About two seconds to free his aching shaft, another second to pull her panties to the side. In less than four seconds he could be thrusting into her intense heat, but Dakota wouldn't be distracted with such ease. An entire life of spiritual practices allowed him to keep his hormones under control...for the most part.

"Wanna play Cowboys and Indians, stud?" She hid behind the bold proposition in an apparent attempt to keep her emotions at bay.

Interesting. Had she unwittingly given him permission for what he knew needed to be done to heal her? His genuine smile lit up the night. "I must warn you, princess...I play for keeps."

"Hmm, well give it your best shot, stud. No man has managed to keep me yet, and I don't see it happening any time in the near future."

Dakota just continued to smile. "We'll see about that, princess. We'll see."

His words seemed to irritate her, and he watched her begin to shut him out, drawing back into herself. The bawdy attitude was definitely a way of shielding herself. He'd have to keep the information in mind.

"Good luck with that!" Rising from his lap, Tamara threw out the challenge and walked away.

He watched the gentle sway of hips until darkness enveloped her. She'd squared her shoulders and stiffened her spine, cloaking herself in a false air of confidence.

Long after the feisty princess had climbed off his lap, he sat thinking about what it would take to bring them together. He had his work cut out for him, but wouldn't let that stop him. If nothing else, Dakota was determined and disciplined enough to make it happen. The only question was how long she'd be able to resist.

Chapter One

The day turned out to be gorgeous, with miles of cloudless blue skies and a gentle breeze. It was a perfect example of why Montana was called "Big Sky Country".

The hands were busy nearby working on various chores. Zeke was in the corral helping with one of the younger fillies while Dakota offered helpful pointers from where he leaned against the fence.

"Getting a feel for an unfamiliar horse is not very different from learning about an unfamiliar person."

Dakota had learned a lot about the horses and ranch hands during the handful of days since coming to the ranch. With Cord and Savannah on their honeymoon everyone was relaxed, and he was able to get a good idea of each person's personality.

He freely shared his vast knowledge about horses as he worked with Zeke. The shy young cowboy seemed to have a true interest in the subject, and enjoyed helping. Too bad he'd be going back to school when the Blacks returned. Two weeks was long enough to learn some of the basics, but he'd miss out on birthing the foals.

"Just being near the animals, observing their actions and reactions, will reveal their personalities." It worked the same with people. In the short time since his arrival, Dakota had learned about Tamara and the other ranch residents through the normal routines of daily ranch life.

"You must be consistent, and allow the animal ample time to learn trust and respect." It was readily apparent Savannah Black had put in a great deal of work with the horses in her breeding program. Each animal was in spectacular physical shape, and well conditioned to accommodate riders of a variety of skill levels, yet still offer a spirited ride.

Zeke digested the information. "Seems reasonable."

Using the same principles and skill, Dakota worked to earn the trust and respect of the ranch hands. This task would take infinite patience. The cowboys of the Shooting Star Ranch were wary of strangers, and his Native American heritage set Dakota that much further apart from them. This wasn't due to any prejudice on their part as much as from the way he embraced his heritage and the spirit of his people, creating a clear difference between them.

Add to this the sexual tension created by a certain princess and his task became much more challenging. Observing Tamara's interactions with the others was enlightening. It was obvious she shared a sexual relationship with the hands. Each of the men went out of his way to draw her attention. The joker of the group, Riley, was the most transparent and many of his pranks were aimed at capturing the aloof woman's focus.

Her focus would soon belong to Dakota and no one else. He harbored no uncertainty Tamara was his spirit mate. One glance into the depths of her green eyes that first night had revealed everything he needed to know. Their interactions since then had cemented his belief.

He was also certain her spirit needed to be healed. The way she flaunted herself and tempted the men didn't fool him. She had some serious scars hidden beneath the attitude. It would require a long, difficult journey to capture her bruised and battered heart.

"The horse will reward the effort by following your commands without resistance or hesitation. Before you win them over, the animal will challenge your authority. Once you pass its tests, a horse will stand true to the connection formed between you."

He loved a good challenge. And what could be better than the task of capturing his princess? Tamara was a free spirit who shied away from any kind of ties or emotion, the very things he needed. It was going to be a tough road to walk.

Spirit mates were bound together tighter than marriage, linked to each other through an ancient, unbreakable bond. His mate would be true to him in her heart, body and mind, sharing every emotion and becoming part of his family without reservations. What a tall order that would be to fill.

The thought of trying to integrate Tamara into his family gave him pause. How would she ever mesh with a group so open to emotion and bound by tradition? She was a loner who did not bind herself to anyone, much less a whole family and culture. The Great Spirit had made sure Dakota had his work cut out for him in claiming his wild mate.

He stared up at the heavens for a moment, wondering if his ancestors were having a good laugh over the seemingly impossible task set before him.

Zeke was quick to catch on to the lesson. "I think I know what you mean. You haven't seen anything until you've seen Van with her big brown stallion, Moon Dancer. He follows her like a puppy and even plays tag with his mistress."

"That's a great example of what I'm talking about. When you form a friendship with a horse, the animal may show facets of its true nature you would never see otherwise." Dakota was anxious to discover his mate's true nature.

As if conjured from his thoughts, Tamara sauntered out the front door of the main house, letting the screen door slam shut with a resounding bang, bringing all ranch work to an abrupt halt. The little minx sure possessed a flair for the dramatic. With practiced nonchalance she tossed her head, sending a curtain of silky hair fanning out around her exotic face.

"Yeehaw," one of the men mumbled in a soft tone.

"Ride 'em, cowgirl." Zeke chuckled as he moved over to where the other hands were working.

Tamara's sheer beauty stole his attention and breath. She possessed a rare magnificence which came from deep within. No matter how hard she tried to hide behind bold actions, her inner beauty shone like a beacon, drawing Dakota in deeper every time he saw her.

A dramatic flick of her wrist and his princess settled a pair of dark sunglasses on her pert nose above strawberry red lips. How he longed to drink from her beautiful mouth.

A soft pink blouse molded to her narrow shoulders, cupping her breasts, drawing attention to enticing curves. The shirt crossed between the two small mounds, clinging to her flesh and seducing the senses, stopping above her navel where a silver piece of jewelry sparkled in the early morning sunlight. He visualized tugging at the hoop with his teeth, dipping his tongue into the shadowed indention.

Painted-on designer jeans rode low on her hips, framing narrow, prominent hip bones he knew would fit within the breadth of his hands. The pink belt she wore was shiny, the buckle covered in rhinestones refracting prisms of light around the yard. She'd tucked the skintight jeans into fancy pink boots, which brought a smile to his lips.

Those boots were not meant for ranch work. They were much better suited as a fashion statement. Hell, he bet she cringed at the thought of walking across the dirty ranch yard in the prissy, expensive footwear.

She moved like gentle waters flowing down stream—smooth and fluid. As she walked to her cabin, Tamara appeared to take no notice of the five men who'd stopped any pretense of work to pay homage to her seductive saunter. Dakota knew better. Her casual disinterest was a calculated facade.

As if the scorching day weren't hot enough already, his mate drove temperatures up to an uncomfortable level with her intense sexuality. Heat surged through Dakota's veins. He wanted Tamara more at that moment than he'd ever desired another woman, but he was going to have to take this at a slow and steady pace if he wanted to win the ultimate prize—her heart.

"Damn, I need to get laid!"

Her entire body visibly tensed when one of the hands made the lewd statement. Still, she did not falter or slow her stride.

Being close to the cabin afforded Dakota with a wonderful vantage point to enjoy the slow sway of her fine ass as she passed by. In his mind's eye, he saw vivid images of her tiny body moving over top of his own, his dark-skinned hands cupping those small, luscious breasts.

All five men were held captive to her seductive spell until the cabin door closed behind her sweet, heart-shaped behind. One of the cowboys groaned, opening quiet discussion between the men as they resumed working when the temptress was out of sight.

The palpable sense of anticipation permeating the yard kept Dakota on the alert. The cowboys were up to something. Riley's expressive face held a sinister grin. Zeke looked worried.

He kept a close eye on the ornery cowboys. They were nice enough toward him on the surface, but he wasn't fooled. Those boys were damned uncomfortable facing an unknown. At times he felt like he was trapped in some corny old western movie where the cowboys would circle their wagons and ready their guns for the attack of the savage Indians.

The other men would have to be blind not to discern Tamara's interest in him. There was a distinct difference in the way she acted when he was around. The minx would toss her hair and laugh out loud in a sexy voice, doing everything possible to draw his attention. It all seemed to make the cowboys feel very nervous and protective. He didn't blame them. Regardless of the tougher-than-nails attitude Tamara portrayed so well, there was no denying the vulnerability she tried to hide. He was glad she had the loyal group of men watching out for her.

Once again, Dakota became lost in the rhythm of the familiar task of grooming the horse. He was pampering Star Gazer today since discovering the big chestnut gelding was favoring one of his legs. While it didn't appear to be anything more serious than an overworked muscle, he was taking no chances. He had already created a healing poultice of special herbs, which now sat on a clay pot absorbing the heat of the sun. When he was done working with Star he would spread the warm substance on a length of cloth, and wrap the affected area.

Tamara's high-pitched, fear-filled scream sliced through the companionable quiet of the ranch yard.

While the cowboys were slow to react, Dakota was over the corral fence in one swift leap, then racing across the short distance. He was just mounting the steps as she flew out the door into his arms, and began climbing him as though he were a tree. She didn't stop until her arms wrapped around his head, holding him in a firm grip, and she was almost sitting on his shoulder. Her entire body trembled against him like a leaf caught in a strong wind.

A small portion of his focus was drawn to the commotion playing out behind his back. Riotous laughter was greeted by a half-hearted curse. "Shit, Riley. What the hell did you do now?" Dakota thought it was Brock who growled the question.

Dakota turned and walked to the main house, stopping at the front porch, where he began the difficult task of peeling one very frightened princess off him. Keeping part of his attention on the cowboys, a clear picture began to take shape. It seemed those boys thought using Tamara's fears was a great way to get her attention.

Millie, the ranch cook, stomped out onto the porch, followed by Craig, the bookkeeper. Millie's wiry gray hair shone almost white in the bright sun, standing out in stark contrast to her deep brown skin. With her hands fisted at her ample hips, the large woman made a quick survey of the scene. Sharp, assessing dark brown eyes took no time at all to figure out what happened.

Craig's young daughter, Mandy, raced around the side of the house and came to a skidding halt at the bottom of the steps. Dakota gave her a reassuring smile to help settle the fear and alarm he sensed rising within the child. He'd been told of her recent trauma from being trapped in a cave by a pedophile, along with Savannah's daring rescue attempt. The girl had made great strides toward resuming a normal life, but became upset if things seemed the least bit dangerous.

It took several minutes to get Tamara settled against the shelter of his chest as Dakota murmured ancient Cheyenne words of comfort. His hands moved in a soothing pattern over her back as she hiccupped and sobbed for several minutes before being able to tell them what happened.

"T-there's a m-mouse...in my cabin. Last time it was a s-snake in the toilet...hooked to fishing string. About scared m-me to death. Cord and Riley had it out. The p-pranks had stopped...until now."

Craig shook his head, while Mandy looked disappointed in the men upon hearing the story. She idolized Riley as her knight in shining armor. Her hurt over his part in scaring Tamara was evident on her sweet face.

"Honey child, you come inside with me now," Millie said, taking hold of Tamara's arm. "I think these boys have a few things to work out, and they don't need you in the middle mucking up the works." She held out a hand to Mandy. "Come on, sugar. I've got a fresh batch of chocolate chip cookies cooling in the kitchen."

While guiding the much smaller woman into the house, Millie shot a penetrating look over her shoulder at Dakota. "I knew those boys would be up to their rowdy tricks with the bossman gone. I'm leavin' this mess with you to sort out, son." Without waiting for a response, she moved her charges into the house.

With a heavy sigh, Dakota headed toward the cabin, doing his best to ignore the other men. He'd already learned his princess held a profound fear of some of nature's smaller creatures. Snakes were at the top of a long list, which included any type of rodent or small, burrowing animals.

What he found in the cabin wasn't much of a surprise. Savannah had forewarned him about Riley's inventive pranks. Even though he saw the humor in the other man's creativity, he wasn't able to forgive Riley for playing on Tamara's fears.

When he'd opened the bedroom door, a small, realistic-looking rubber mouse scurried across the wooden floor. On closer inspection, he found fishing line trailing from the bottom corner of the door to the rodent, rigged in such a way that when the door was opened it pulled the mouse across its path.

Under other circumstances he would have chuckled, but protective instincts made his blood boil. A violent rage tested the limits of his calm spirit. For the first time in his memory, Dakota felt like causing harm to another. Set up for anyone else it would have been a funny prank. Sprung on someone with known fears of such creatures, it was downright cruel.

Snapping the line, Dakota reeled in the rubber rodent and let it hang from his fist. Turning on his heel, he faced the four cowboys who waited inside the front door. They all stood with a deliberate air of calm, a casual relaxation in their stance, with the exception of Zeke. He appeared to be experiencing genuine upset over what had happened. Brock wore an expression of passive acceptance. Riley and Jesse, the smug look of little boys basking in the glow of success from a great prank having been sprung with success. Although, Dakota was certain they would have been happier with the results if Tamara had flown into one of their embraces instead of his.

He knew every one of them cared for Tamara, yet they turned a blind eye, accepting the brassy, free-spirited front she put on. Not one of them took the time to take a closer look at the woman and find out what made her tick. They didn't allow themselves to see her dissatisfaction with life in general or make the effort to help her change things.

The four men watched his every move, anticipated his reaction and waited for a big scene, but Dakota would not be giving it to them. Let them get their cheap jollies at someone else's expense. They had been trying to provoke a response from him since his arrival, but he would not give them the satisfaction of playing into their game.

A visible tension rippled through each man as he walked toward the front door, making his way out of the cabin without a word, dropping the fake mouse into a wastebasket along the way. While he wanted to go and provide comfort to Tamara, he returned to the corral instead. After picking up the clay pot, Dakota resumed tending to the horse.

Using a wooden spatula, he began to spread the thick poultice onto a long, thin strip of muslin. He snuck surreptitious glances from the corner of his eye as the cowboys began to file back out of the cabin and return to their work. It was obvious they were disturbed by his lack of rejoinder to their antics. Even Brock, the most levelheaded of the group, seemed to be perplexed.

Wiping the back of his hand across his mouth, Dakota was able to hide his grin. He refused to fit in to the niche the Shooting Star's cowboys had picked out for him, having no intention of making things easy for them. He could almost see the wheels turning as they puzzled out ways to get a reaction out of him. It was apparent they were not used to dealing with someone who possessed any amount of self-control.

The hands kept a close watch on him as he went about his business of working with the horse. Not a moment went by he didn't feel their eyes watching every move he made.

As things returned to a normal rhythm, everyone began to relax. He sensed the plotting going on, and instinct told him the focus of the pranksters would be turning toward him. Good. Better him than Tamara, even though Dakota knew the less response they were able to get out of him, the more dramatic the stunts would become. Things were going to be very interesting until the hands became accustomed to his ways.

Scorching hot rays of summer sun beat down on them as they went about their work. Before long, shirts were plastered to sweaty bodies. When Dakota removed the offensive garment, he felt the other men sizing him up. Although he was only as tall as the shortest of the cowboys, his well-developed muscles and dark coloring along with his controlled presence made him appear much larger.

With an inward chuckle, he wondered when the measuring stick would be pulled out. The pissing contest was already well underway, regardless if he refused to play.

CR80

Taking a deep breath, Tamara allowed the tension to seep out of her body as she sat talking with Millie in the kitchen. Everyone else had gone back to what they'd been doing before the drama had unfolded.

"Riley gets me with those damn childish pranks every time."

"And he'll keep at it," Millie said. "Long as you keep reacting, he'll keep prankin' you. That cowboy wants your attention and this is the most sure fire way to get it."

What she said made sense. In the short time since the older woman had come to the ranch, Millie had become the mother Tamara had never known. She felt comforted by being in the other woman's presence. The sage advice Millie dished out along with her wonderful culinary creations had already proved useful on several occasions.

"At least I got cookies out of it." Tamara's wide grin made Millie chuckle like she'd hoped it would. "So how do I get him to stop?"

"I'm not sure he will stop since you've been paying so much attention to Dakota." Tamara started to object, but Millie held her hand up and kept talking. "Don't try to deny it, honey child. The heat between you two is enough to light the burner on the stove."

Tamara snorted. "That obvious, huh?"

"Only to anyone with eyes."

"What that smartass Riley has yet to realize is he's cost the whole lot of them any of my attention." At least until she no longer was able to withstand the build-up of sexual energy. And if or when she decided to let them fuck her again, Tamara had every intention of making them work for it.

The very idea brought a wicked smile to her face. Those boys had no idea what they were in for. Yet for some reason the idea of fucking the cowboys no longer held the same appeal it once had. How strange.

"Things are going to change around here, Millie. Those boys will have to find someone else to mess with."

And damn the super calm, know-it-all Dakota. She had expected a reaction similar to Cord's pissed-off mood when the cowboys played tricks on her, but when she glanced out the window, surveying the men working in the yard, no one had a black eye and everything seemed peaceful.

Too damn peaceful.

"It's awfully quiet out there."

"I imagine Dakota has his own way of handlin' things. He's more subtle than Cord, less in your face."

Well, she'd stir things up soon enough.

"How do I handle them now, Millie?"

"Best thing you can do is not react the way those boys are waiting for. Show them the games aren't working and they'll

33

have to change their tactics. And most important, never let them see ya sweat, honey child."

It was a good plan. She would show a cool, calm and collected front the men would not expect possible after their prank. It would eat them up wondering why she wasn't upset.

Standing inside the house, she prepared herself for the walk across the yard, replaying Millie's advice in her mind. With nary a whisper of sound, she opened the door and headed across the porch, making a quick mental note of the men's activities.

When she caught sight of Dakota working in the corral, she almost fell down the steps, catching herself at the last moment before tumbling ass over teakettle into the yard. The glorious sight would forever be burned into her memory. Although she'd dated some very gorgeous men over the years, nothing prepared her for the sight of a shirtless Dakota Blackhawk.

"Good gravy."

The man was a work of art suitable of gracing a lighted pedestal in the most impressive gallery. Perspiration glistened along dark cinnamon skin, which held a glow from healthy living. Not an inch of the man was lacking in well-defined muscle. Strength and vitality seeped from every pore of his hard body. She found it impossible to imagine a more perfect male specimen.

It was difficult to not outright stare at the miles of rippling sinew creating such a wonderful display of masculinity. Light and shadow melded in a magical dance over each glorious curve and angle across massive shoulders, wide chest, and impressive abdomen. She would find it easy to lose herself for weeks tracing each powerful arc and crease, tasting each beautiful inch of dark skin.

He turned toward the horse he was working with, giving her an unobstructed view of flexing muscles working across a very broad back. His shiny blue-black hair was wrapped in a thong, creating a short tail, which swished down between those drool-worthy shoulders she longed to nibble on.

A tattooed chain of small black ovals ringed his left arm. As he'd turned once again, she followed the chain as it melded with perfection into the seam between sinews, connected on the front of his biceps by twin feathers dangling down over thick male flesh. Hell if it wasn't the hottest tattoo she'd ever seen, perfectly suited to the man it graced.

Drinking in the sight of his delicious pecs, garnished with flat brown nipples riding low on the outer edge of each defined muscle, she found herself wondering what would please this man. Would he enjoy having his nipples licked, nibbled, teased? Would he enjoy the warm slide of her tongue as she laved each yummy slat over his washboard abdomen, dipping into the dark, shadowed navel?

The faded jeans he wore didn't do much to disguise the massive accumulation of muscle gracing long, thick legs. She felt an insatiable curiosity to discover if there were any more tattoos adorning his magnificent body, and if what looked to be a very large package was even half as impressive as the rest of him.

When she climbed into the driver's seat of her Jeep and shut the door, Tamara released the pent up breath she'd not even been aware of holding. Under normal circumstances her cowboys would have held her undivided attention, but they never even entered her mind as she'd crossed the yard. Every iota of her conscious thought had been locked on Dakota, wiping everyone and everything else from existence.

With her sheer grit and indomitable spirit firmly back in place, Tamara gunned the Jeep and headed out to seize the bull by the horns. She was one pit bull of a cowgirl who would not turn loose until the final buzzer rang declaring her the victor. And she planned to ride this wild bull to win. She began the careful contemplation and plotting of what it would take to bring down the very calm, unflappable horseman.

"Get ready, cowboy. It's gonna be a wild ride."

For right now though, she felt like going a good ten rounds with Jose Cuervo while devising the downfall of one Dakota Blackhawk.

Instead of tying one on, Tamara headed to town and her saving grace, Paperback Roundup. The bookstore may be small, but she was proud to be its owner. More than any other activity, sharing her love of books allowed her to relax and clear her mind. She needed the time and distraction to consider everything Millie said and to get her head back on straight.

Starting an after school program for the local kids had not been planned. It began with one curious girl who'd reminded Tamara of herself. Emily had asked for help picking out a book and they'd started discussing different stories. The next day Emily brought a friend along and word quickly spread around their school. Before long there was a large group gathering at the store each weekday afternoon.

She prayed the cowboys never found out because they'd tease her without mercy. The program was a total contradiction to the woman they knew. Thankfully, Savannah had kept her secret and salvaged the hard-ass rep she maintained at the ranch. And the guys didn't go into town often during the week, much less stop by the bookstore, to find out about it on their own.

Being able to provide a safe place for the kids to pass the time between school and their parents getting home from work made her feel like she made a difference in their lives. Everyone took turns bringing snacks and she didn't charge a fee to be a member of the book club. The service was her way of giving back to the townspeople who'd so readily accepted both Tamara and her store. Besides, what she got in return far outweighed the expenditure of time and resources.

To witness a child's eyes light up over an intriguing story warmed her heart and provided the sense of accomplishment she'd lacked. The way they looked up to her and asked her opinion filled her with joy. It was cute the way they called her Miss Tamara, too.

Yes, the store and the kids were exactly what she needed.

Chapter Two

After breakfast the next morning, Dakota watched Tamara move out to the front porch with a cup of coffee. The time she'd spent in town seemed to have calmed her after the previous day's drama. He filled a mug and joined her. The mountain views from the main house were spectacular. There wasn't a better setting for a nice chat.

It had become a daily ritual for the two of them to sit together and talk over coffee since he'd moved to the ranch. Each day brought them closer together as they opened up and shared more of their lives.

He watched her through the screen door for a moment before making his presence known. She kept fidgeting, unable to sit still and enjoy the peaceful morning. He'd noticed before how antsy she got when alone, and wanted to find out why.

Dakota was moving a bit slow. His hip was sore from performing dressage training with a particularly stubborn horse the day before. He kept the injury a secret for the most part, not wanting the others to treat him differently or question his capability due to the physical deficiency. It was also a matter of his pride, and rivalry with the cowboys. Only the ranch owners, and Steph since she'd been there during his interview, were aware of his limitations.

"It's a beautiful morning."

"A little too quiet for me. I prefer when the boys are working around the yard." She gave him a quizzical glance. "Why are you limping today?"

Dakota brushed the question off without giving specifics. "It's nothing. My muscles are kind of sore." He'd rather get her talking about herself than discuss his injury.

When he sat down they were close together, but with a small gap between their bodies. He figured it must be adequate personal space for her since she didn't tense up.

"Quiet mornings like this always remind me of my grandmother. She enjoyed watching the sunrise and a new day begin. Since I was an early riser, it became our special time. We didn't talk. Just sat and watched the world wake up."

"Sounds boring."

"It was relaxing—a way to center myself, but what I really enjoyed was being with my family. We are very close and there's always someone around to pass the time with. Brothers and sisters, cousins, nieces and nephews. Many of them still keep their families together. I'm one of the few who has wandered away in search of my future."

She seemed to contemplate what having a big family would be like. Dakota had told her stories of growing up with a large family. He hoped it was getting easier for Tamara to understand the companionship since it was essential to him. He was sure she didn't realize it wasn't that different from what she had with her ranch family.

"I had two worlds to explore—the reservation and the city. My parents made sure I learned the ways of both cultures. There were quiet times alone, and playful times filled with love. I hope to give my own kids a similar childhood."

He searched for a way to keep Tamara at ease and draw her out. Tales of childhood dreams and discoveries brought a wistful expression to her face.

"I bet you shared a similar experience with your foster families, Tamara."

The lack of humor in her laughter made Dakota's heart ache for his princess. He knew her life had been hard. If she'd talk to him, perhaps he'd be able to ease some of her hurt.

"You didn't share quiet times together?"

"Nah. Usually wasn't around long enough to get close to anyone. Moved from one foster home to another. Only ever had myself. Before I was even a teenager, I learned the harsh realities of life and how to take care of myself."

Ah. The information brought some of her personality into perspective, but he needed to keep her talking.

"You were so young. How did you take care of yourself? Isn't that what the foster parents were there for?"

She stared off into the distance and seemed to travel back in time.

"Not all foster families are good, although I did live with some nice people. Some are in it for the check they get from the state each month. I learned to use my wits to fend off those with a size and strength advantage. When wielded with care and skill, sex could be used to obtain what you needed. Essentials like protection, security, food and a good night's sleep."

His heart broke for what she'd gone through as a child. Hardship and pain had shaped the woman she was today. No child should have to use her body to obtain the basic comforts. He asked a general question to keep her talking. "A good night's sleep?"

"Yeah, sleep. I didn't get a lot of that after I moved in with the Rubins when I was twelve. Stayed with them until I was finally able to take off by myself. The parents were alcoholics, the foster kids their own personal slaves. We worked the kennels where they bred vile dogs." Tamara shivered, and he moved closer.

"I was terrified of those snarling, drooling beasts, but found out there are far worse things in life. Like the Rubins' son, Steve. He was one sick bastard."

"What was so bad about Steve?"

For several heartbeats she remained quiet. He knew she didn't talk about the past often, and he had to tread carefully. If he pushed too hard, she'd clam up. It was best to let her tell the story at her own pace so he waited her out.

"Steve was the enforcer who kept the foster kids toeing the line by using terror, physical threat and cruel pranks. He's the kind of kid who grows up to be a serial rapist and killer. The bastard enjoyed catching and torturing small animals, then he'd intimidate the rest of us with them. Learned the hard way to check my bed before sliding beneath the covers, and to examine my shoes before putting them on. Nothing worse than bare feet hitting sticky blood and guts. If Steve thought you had not done enough work, or if you stood up to his bullying, some poor creature paid the price.

"His dad was even worse. In the middle of the night, when it was nice and quiet, Aaron Rubin would stumble drunkenly into my bedroom. I wasn't strong enough to fight him off." She wrapped her arms around her slender body.

"The horrible stench of alcohol on his breath turned my stomach and I had to struggle to keep my dinner down as his dirty hands pulled at my skin."

41

She stopped talking again, lost in thought. The reality of her childhood was worse than he'd anticipated. That she'd survived was a testament to her strength and will, but she hadn't escaped without scars.

"Aaron's wife didn't stop him?"

"Gail was passed out long before he came to me. Steve caught him one night, dragged the bastard off. I foolishly hoped it was over, but Steve came back to finish what his father had started. He threatened me with horrific punishments to keep me from telling my social worker."

His heart ached for the girl who had suffered so much. Tamara seemed to realize how much she'd revealed and suddenly jumped up from the swing, shutting him out.

"Fucking hell! I don't want to talk about the past. It's best left forgotten." She got up and stalked away, clearly upset by her memories.

Tamara pulled herself together. She was way out of her element with Dakota. All her life lessons in dealing with men went right out the window whenever he was near. A frightening prospect indeed. She'd have to be careful in his presence. His calm voice and soothing tone lulled her into a false sense of security.

What the hell was drawing her to him? She didn't understand. They were poles apart and needed different things. He thrived on sharing emotions and required a sense of community which, in her mind, restricted freedom, tying a person irrevocably to others.

Dakota was into the whole one-man-one-woman, happily-ever-after scenario. She knew fairytale bullshit like that wasn't possible. None of it jibed with her, yet there was this unseen factor pulling her to him. Like an adrenaline junky drawn to the next life-threatening thrill.

Tamara wouldn't run. She hated to be alone. Plus she had to be at the ranch to work with Steph and Jesse on designing a website for Paperback Roundup. For the time being, though, she put some distance between herself and Dakota, leaving him to his work and diving into her own.

CR80

Later that day, warm afternoon sunshine shed new light on his work. Dakota stood by the fence, an unobtrusive presence observing the energetic play of a filly as she pranced around the corral. It had not been a full week since his arrival at the ranch, yet each day the tan Buckskin moved further into season. The signs were all there. It was time to test Honey's receptiveness to being mated.

Her coloring was exceptional, showing all the classic Dun markings of the breed. She even had a dark brown dorsal strip running the length of her spine. These markings, accompanied by her dark mane, tail, forelegs and tipped ears made Honey a beautiful specimen.

She was to be mated with Rowdy, a red Dun stallion. With his reddish-tan coat and shaded markings similar to Honey's, the paring had the potential to produce a gorgeous foal. Buckskins were known for their endurance, stamina, versatile nature, disposition and beautiful color. The strength and tenacity of the breed, relative to its size, made it popular for rodeo work and cattle ranching.

This particular foal, if the mating was successful, would be headed to the rodeo. The buyer who had commissioned the mating was purchasing the animal in anticipation of his son following in his footsteps on the circuit.

While Dakota appreciated the hard work and sportsmanship of the rodeo as well as the next person, he hated the way it consumed a man's soul. Having witnessed the shattered lives of those who went down the path, he knew firsthand about the heartbreak of the rodeo. More than a few who participated were possessed by the call of the wild competition and potential for fame and glory. In reality, very few made it to the top rankings.

What he despised most was the way competitors left their families behind to follow the circuit and how it controlled their very existence. It was a difficult life filled with the pain of broken bones, hearts shred to pieces, and shattered lives. However, it wasn't his plight to worry about. His job was to ensure a successful mating, the safety of the horses, and delivery of a champion quality foal.

"Good morning."

He felt Steph's quiet presence before seeing her approach the corral fence where he stood. Cord Black's younger sister presented a soft, quiet appearance to the world. For the most part this was an accurate view of the beautiful woman, but not the complete picture. Beneath the exterior lurked the spirit of an adventurer.

Dakota could easily picture the curvy woman getting into a lot of trouble exploring the world when she was a child. If one looked close enough into the depths of those blue-gray eyes, it was possible to catch a glimpse of the precocious girl anxious for the next marvelous escapade.

An immediate kinship had developed between them. Dakota had been happy to find talking things out with Stephanie and answering her questions often helped him to decide on the best course of action. He welcomed a conversation with the inquisitive beauty as enthusiastically as he welcomed the rising sun beginning each new day. Her spirit was gentle and life affirming, like the first dazzling morning rays to kiss the land.

"Good morning," Steph said in her shy tone. "I'm not interrupting, am I?"

With a genuine smile lighting his face, Dakota turned to her, opening his arms. "Not at all, sunshine." They shared a brief embrace before returning their attention to the horse. "I do believe Honey," he said, nodding toward the mare, "is almost ready to be mated."

Glancing over at Steph, he basked in the changes overtaking her sweet face. Here was something new to discover. Her eyes sparkled with intelligence, and he saw the gears turning as she formed her first questions.

"How does the horse reveal that it's time?"

Leaning his forearms on the rail, Dakota began to explain the mating process and observable signs to know when the time was right for the animal. As he spoke, Brock appeared from the stable leading Rowdy. Following Dakota's prior instructions, Brock walked the horse in a path around the corral, while still keeping some distance from the fence.

It didn't take long for Honey to pick up the stallion's scent, and vice versa. The golden filly stopped her prancing and sniffed the air.

"See how, without hesitation, Honey raises her tail, holding it to the left, in a classic mating posture? She's letting Rowdy know she's ready," Dakota pointed out. "Think of it as similar to when a woman swings her head, flipping her hair to draw a man's attention."

From watching Rowdy, it was clear the big stallion was putting Brock through the paces, yet the cowboy's calm, casual appearance did not reflect the fact the horse was testing his mettle. Brock kept Rowdy under control and walking at the pace he set as they made a wide loop around the corral.

"Brock has his work cut out for him in keeping Rowdy under control. The stallion has a one-track mind right now, and it's focused on getting to the female. You can also tell the female's attention is on attracting the big stud."

Honey's gaze followed the other horse's slow progress, itching to get closer to Rowdy. The whole time, Dakota kept up a running dialogue with Steph, explaining what was happening.

"In essence, the horses are flirting with each other, letting it be known they are receptive to the pairing." While talking, he took in everything happening around them.

"What happens next?" Steph asked, excitement dripping from her voice.

As Brock and Rowdy passed behind them, Dakota called out instructions for Brock to walk the stallion around the corral one more lap, then stop when he again reached where they stood.

"Next we bring them closer together. Give them a little time to communicate." Dakota gave Steph instructions to keep her safe when the horses were brought together. Even though Rowdy had a calm disposition, it was difficult to predict if the cowboys would be able to keep control of him when he got close to a receptive female. "I want you to move away from the fence, nice and slow. Step back toward the road, giving me at least fifty feet to work so I don't have to worry about you."

The animals called to each other as Brock walked the stallion around the corral for the second time. Dakota watched to make sure Steph followed his directives as Brock and Rowdy approached the spot where Dakota stood at the fence.

"This is Honey's first time going into season and her first mating experience," he said, speaking louder now. "She's showing an appropriate level of excitement and skittishness at the same time." He kept a close eye on both the animals and his assistant. "Rowdy, on the other hand, is well accustomed to the process."

The stallion was ready to mate—his member extended hard and long from his body, ball sac drawn tight and close. Brock kept rigid control over the big animal to make sure things did not turn ugly, and Rowdy acted like a gentleman.

"Notice the care Rowdy takes when coming close," Dakota commented. The wise stallion approached the fence with an air of ease and confidence, assessing the signs of Honey's acceptance. His heavy hooves dug into the soft earth in his barely leashed excitement to join with the filly. As he reached the fence, the two animals began to sniff and nuzzle each other.

Dakota kept a close watch on both animals, along with a constant stream of dialogue for both Brock and Steph, delivered in a soothing monotone. "Honey is now flashing her vulva repeatedly, squirting copious fluids, and holding a mating stance. It's important to make sure all the signs are present, and are clearly noticeable.

"Honey is ready, and appears to be receptive to the idea of allowing Rowdy to mount her. It's time for final preparations." Dakota nodded toward Brock. "Let's move to the next stage."

Steph stayed at the edge of the road where she was out of the way and safe from harm. As the cowboy led the stallion back into the stables, Dakota moved into the corral with Honey. He continued to talk in soothing tones to the big animal while attaching a lead to her halter. "I'll spend a few minutes walking her around the corral now. This will give Brock time to get Rowdy settled into his stall."

When Zeke appeared to signal him, Dakota led Honey into the opposite end of the stable from where Rowdy had entered. Both horses would now go through last minute preparations. When he moved back over to the corral, he explained the process to Steph, speaking loud enough for her to hear him from where she stood.

"Each animal's genitals are being washed with warm water in an attempt to minimize the insertion of dirt and dead skin during the mating. Honey's tail will be wrapped tight in plastic and secured to prevent it from getting in the way."

"Why can't the horses just be put in the corral and let nature take its course?" Steph asked.

"There are many things that can go wrong during natural mating. The filly may become fickle and decide she in fact does not like the stallion—regardless that she is in full heat. The stallion can become nasty or aggressive and scratch up the mare's back. Brock will remain in control, handling Rowdy, and insuring the randy stud does not cause any injuries. Zeke will help Honey through the mating."

Dakota longed to be the one handling Rowdy through this process, but was physically limited by his hip injuries. It rankled not to be able to complete a task he'd participated in many times before. The remembered pain of pushing himself too hard previously held him in check. He had no desire to put himself at risk of another dislocation.

Zeke stood nearby putting on soft deerskin work gloves. He would be handling the mare—helping to hold her in position and providing support as the stallion mounted her.

Dakota explained, "I've worked with both men to make sure they're able to handle the dangerous joining of two large animals." He was happy to see Zeke followed his advice, donning a riding helmet to protect his head since he would be positioned near the stallion's hooves.

A whirlwind of dust and the roar of a motor were all the advanced warning of impending disaster Dakota had. Pivoting, he raced to where Steph stood at the edge of the road. With her attention focused on the horses, she hadn't noticed the danger to herself. He grabbed her around the waist, pulling her close against him and out of the speeding vehicle's path as it flew by, spraying gravel over them in its wake.

"Fuck," he grumbled. The last thing he needed was some reckless fool spooking the horses at a critical time like this.

Still holding Steph sheltered against his body, he turned to see Tamara step down out of her Jeep. She swung her head, tossing her dark hair in a way which reminded him of Honey leading the stallion into the mating dance. Damn, the hellion was really pushing the limits of his patience with her crazy antics.

He was conflicted, vacillating between red hot anger and blazing desire. No matter how reckless she acted, he wanted her with a blind passion, almost to the exclusion of everything else.

Dakota struggled to maintain his inner calm as she flashed him a wicked, flirtatious grin. The spitfire had intended to startle them, yet under her attitude he sensed both anger and hurt. Something had upset his princess, and he was almost certain the cause was jealousy over Steph grasping his biceps as she struggled to get her breathing under control.

Tamara wore a sheepish look as she walked over, and shot a worried glance at Steph. Seeing him hold another woman close and focusing on her was obviously irritating to Tamara, but he thought she was sorry for her actions. Still, she brought out the brassy attitude.

"What's wrong with kid sister? Something scare ya?"

The taunting words were filled with her own hurt. She didn't like being ignored, and her actions had not brought about quite the reaction she had hoped for. Tamara had only managed to drive Steph into his arms, instead of further away, and ensured she remained the center of his attention.

"That's quite enough." Dakota spoke in a slow, even tone. Reaching out, he ran his fingers in a gentle trail down the frightened girl's cheek while gazing into her eyes. "Okay, sunshine?"

He admired Steph's strength as she pulled herself together, stepping back from his embrace. She would not reprimand Tamara for her thoughtless actions. Instead she brushed the dust off her clothes and straightened her shoulders.

"Yes, I'm fine. I think I'll head back inside and get some work done now. Thanks for explaining about the horses, Dakota." She gave him a bright smile, ignoring the other woman's presence as she headed across the yard.

He felt the resentment rolling off his princess in waves. It was blatantly obvious she was none too happy he and Steph had become friends. Everyone on the ranch had picked up on her tension whenever Steph was anywhere near him. To have her stunt backfire and drive Steph into his embrace was probably too much for her. Well good, let her stew in the results of her actions for a bit.

Dakota turned from Tamara as Zeke led Honey into the corral. The two took up their position and waited for Rowdy. They would wait several minutes before bringing out the stallion for everyone's protection. Keeping the big animal calm was paramount to their success.

As Dakota took up his position along the fence, Tamara gave a disgruntled "harrumph". For a brief moment she had considered running over the woman, but it was difficult to lash out at Steph. Cord's sister was such a genuine, likeable person, but she was also too smart and beautiful for her own good.

Damn, Tamara really had to shut down whatever the hell was going on with her. Seeing Steph talking with Dakota had put her into some kind of conniption fit. Something about the sweet, smart-assed bitch made her plunge into insanity in two point four seconds flat.

Of course, it wasn't jealousy. She almost snorted at the very idea. *Pshaw, like I'd be jealous of precious Stephanie.* Tamara wouldn't allow herself to feel useless emotions like those. And there was no way she was envious of Cord's brainy sister. No freakin' way in hell! The woman was sweet enough to induce a diabetic coma.

Having things sorted out in her mind allowed her to breathe a little easier. Now she'd be able to focus on the big man who was driving her to distraction.

"What's going on?" she asked, moving in close to Dakota's side. For a moment he didn't respond and she was afraid she'd pissed him off with her actions. *Damn, psycho. Congratulations. You royally screwed the pooch.*

After some time, he nodded toward the mare. "Honey has gone into season and is about to be mated for the first time with one of the stallions."

It was obvious by the look on Dakota's face this was a major event for him. She felt a slight pang of regret over the way she'd behaved. It would have been terrible of her to mess this up for him. Damn, why were her emotions so out of control around this man? She'd never experienced anything quite like these feelings before. Her normal attitude toward men was reticent at best. This was quite different and out of her experience.

Somehow, this man touched a part of her she'd managed to keep cold, indifferent and shut-off for many years. She had no idea what it was about the big Indian that sparked such passion in her. Merely listening to him talk about the most mundane subject made her squirm. There was something about his deep voice and the sexy cadence of his speech that made her knees feel weak, her body needy.

She had vivid memories of sitting on the swing with him one morning as Dakota talked about his childhood. She'd been saddened to hear the things ignorant people had whispered about him, looking down on the small, innocent boy because his father was a cowboy and his mother Native American. People were so cruel, especially to children or those who were weaker and smaller. Still, he hadn't let it leave a sour taste in his mouth.

He'd grown up with a blending of both cultures. She figured he would be able to fit in anywhere with relative ease. The man had such an easygoing nature. Merely standing next to him made her feel calm, soothed. Made her think about having a home, setting down roots. Raising a family and being connected to others. As if!

Feeling these unwanted emotions was not good. They made her long for things she would never have. Common, everyday desires she didn't want to experience. She didn't want to have a craving for some pie-in-the-sky concepts she knew did not exist. Not for her at least. Yet apparently, they were important to him.

When Brock came into view with Rowdy, he had threaded a chain lead line through the lower half of the halter. It was an extra safety precaution, giving him some added leverage should he need to quickly gain the stallion's attention if Rowdy started to misbehave.

When Tamara looked over at Dakota, she again felt a soul-deep longing for the man who called to her in ways she'd never imagined possible. It didn't matter she knew so little about the stoic man or the fact they were such opposites.

He seemed to love spending time alone in peaceful contemplation and maintained such a calm demeanor and presence. She hated being alone, confronted by unwanted sentiment, and was about as far from calm as a person could get. No, he was nothing like her at all and far from the normal bad boy type for whom she held an endless, fatal attraction.

With a deep sigh he moved behind her, boxing her between the fence and the steel bands of his arms as his hands held a firm grasp on the top rung. The warmth of his big body enveloped her. Tamara felt a heated flush rise from her breasts and over her neck to settle high on her cheeks. It took every ounce of willpower she possessed to keep from leaning back against him, luxuriating in his presence surrounding her.

His breath created a hot caress against her ear as he leaned forward and began speaking. The sexy, raspy baritone slid over her skin like heated molasses, slow and sensual. "Watch them, princess."

The firm caress of his lips brushing against the shell of her ear made her breasts feel heavy, achy, her cunt warm and wet. The whisper of his breath over her neck made her body shudder.

Fucking need to get laid. And soon!

"You can tell the female is ready to be mounted. Her cunt is swollen. See how her hot juices slide from her vagina in anticipation of taking the stallion's big shaft. She wants him. Every muscle is tensed as she waits for him to come to her, to fill her up."

Oh shit! How about filling me up, stud? She had no problem imagining how the horse felt. Tamara was reacting the same way as Honey—flesh quivering, pussy lips swollen and dripping—wet and ready. If only she were able to have an enjoyable experience with one man, but she knew better. For her, orgasm required more stimulation than one cock was capable of delivering. All of her attempts at one-on-one sex in the recent past had left her frustrated. She was not able to get off anymore without at least three big cocks fucking all her orifices at once.

Her body readied itself anyway, betraying Tamara and confusing her jumbled thoughts. Her breasts were so full, needy. It took all her self-control to keep her hands on the fence rail and not rub the small globes or tweak her peaked nipples. Dakota's heady, masculine scent enveloping her made her clit pulse. The silky material of her panties flooded with her cream, the scent of arousal rising on the heated air between them.

"She wants this, weeps for it." Dakota whispered the words against her ear.

Tamara watched as Brock walked the big stallion into the corral at a measured pace, keeping the horse under his rigid command. She tried to keep the animals at the center of her attention instead of the big man behind her. She made a concerted effort to keep her breathing steady so he wouldn't know how much his words and actions affected her, but a knot of sexual need twisted her stomach as she watched the horse pace close behind the mare.

She felt Dakota moving, the heat of his body warming her back, intense sexual energy crowding her closer to the fence. Tamara was certain his actions would mirror those of the stallion's cautious yet eager approach to the filly.

"You can feel the stallion's anticipation of shafting the mare—see it in the trembling of his body. He can smell the scent of her need as her body prepares itself for him. He knows she is wet and all he has to do is mount her from behind, sliding his huge cock into her slick, ready passage."

Hell fucking yeah, she screamed within her head.

Tamara stifled an inward groan as Dakota's thick erection pressed against the crevice of her ass, hot and insistent. He was so wonderfully hard and long. Her legs became weak as he rocked against her. She couldn't resist pushing back into the harder-than-steel length of his questing shaft or take her eyes off the scene taking place in the corral before them.

Brock led the stallion toward the mare at an angle, not allowing the horse to mount right away. He kept the stallion far enough away from the mare so all the horse managed to do was extend his neck over and nuzzle her genitals.

Fuck! That had to feel good.

Dakota continued to speak against her ear, sending tingling currents of electricity through her entire body. Right then she would have risked everything to feel his mouth teasing her wet folds, his tongue lapping at her inflamed clit.

"First he will taste her desire, let it roll around on his tongue and fill him with her essence. He'll lap up as much of that sweet cream as he can, teasing the mare. Make her long for what only he can give her."

The wet swipe of the stallion's big tongue over Honey's sensitive folds had the horse screaming out in need. Tamara felt an echo of the same need ooze from her sensitive skin as Dakota continued to rock his erection into the crease of her ass.

He felt better than good. He felt like something she needed with a desperation bordering on obsession. She wanted nothing more than to drop her jeans, spread her legs and impale herself on his thick length. Have every hard inch filling her all the way to her empty heart.

"See the way Honey's muscles ripple beneath her skin as she anticipates Rowdy's long cock ramming into her? She wants to feel him pounding into her hot cunt, stroking her sensitive walls."

Hell yes she saw it. She shared Honey's eagerness to experience such a glorious impalement. Dakota created a longing in her well beyond anything in her experience. It burned through her body with an incomprehensible molten desire.

They watched as Zeke braced the mare, providing a bit of physical support as the stallion mounted her, his forelegs and chest resting over her back. The stud looked downright primal, single-minded in his desire to mate. He rutted around until he was properly aligned with the mare then slid forward, driving his shaft into her body, his teeth nipping at her neck. Animal grunts and cries of passion rose in the air.

At the same time, Dakota thrust his cock against her ass, his teeth capturing the tender flesh where neck and shoulder meet. Tamara's eyes clamped shut as carnal wants flooded her system. The words he spoke between swipes of his tongue over the pulse point in her neck were lost in her lust-fogged mind. She dissolved into a mass of quivering, hypersensitive nerve endings.

Time lost all meaning for Tamara. She had no idea how long she stood there with the big stud rocking against her ass. All she knew was she desired him more than she ever had any other man. Yet desire wasn't quite right. This reaction was much more, reaching toward becoming an all-consuming requirement. She needed his cock filling her, making her complete.

She was astonished to find watching two horses fuck, combined with Dakota's words, was turning her on so much. More than any porno flick ever had. As the stallion groaned out his satisfaction, Dakota's moan filled her ear.

"I want you so much, princess."

Hell yes!

Tamara was ready to scream out her answer when her eyes snapped wide open, drawn to the tableau in the corral. It was over already. Brock led the stallion away as Zeke began walking the mare around the ring, not allowing her to stop. The combined ejaculate from the animals dripped down the mare's legs, like her own cream was coating Tamara's thighs.

The other thing capturing her attention was the knowing look on Zeke's handsome face. The smug bastard stared at the two of them as though they were buck naked and fucking right there in the middle of the yard for all to see. She read a lot of things in his expression. Jealousy, desire and...relief? Why the hell would he be relieved to see Dakota taking an interest in her? Maybe the perverted freak wanted to watch?

The very idea snapped her back to reality. She would not stand here and allow herself to be bombarded by unwanted emotion. She made a forceful thrust against Dakota. He had not anticipated the movement, his surprise allowing her to drive him backward. When she twirled around on her heels, she swallowed a startled gasp.

Holy hell. The man was so breathtaking her knees shook, testing her ability to stand, along with her resistance. His black hair had fallen free of its binding and now hung in a silky mane around his head and shoulders. His face was full of sexual promise, lips somewhat parted, eyes heavy lidded, pupils dilated.

If the heated pheromones radiating off his big body were not enough, the primal look on his face alone would have stopped her cold. It would be so easy to succumb to the desire in his gaze, drag him into her cabin and ride him until they both achieved release, but it wasn't going to happen. She'd be left even more frustrated than she already felt because one-on-one wouldn't do it for her.

Well, fuck a damn duck.

Without a word she brushed past him, struggling not to run, moving with a smooth fluidity which defied the trembling in her legs. She needed to put some distance between them, and a cold shower was sounding pretty damn good right about now. The day had turned out to be a scorcher in more ways than one. She needed to find a way to douse these flames before she combusted.

Chapter Three

All he could do was stay rooted to the spot and watch her walk away. With every fiber of his being, Dakota wanted to go after her. His randy cock wanted nothing more than to sink into the wet velvet glove between her legs, knowing she would grasp him like a hot, tight fist.

Taking her wasn't about to happen any time soon though. Not until Tamara's spirit was healed and she was able to accept everything he had to offer. They would both suffer until she opened her heart to his love.

Getting them both worked up had probably not been a great idea with no relief in sight. His engorged, aching cock wasn't going to help him get his job done.

It didn't matter he had participated in mating horses many times before, something about watching the event with Tamara had taken away the clinical aspect, making it a sensual experience. He'd come very close to ripping and clawing the clothes from her body, releasing his dick, and slamming it into the warm haven of her pussy. Breathing in the musky scent of her arousal had driven away all higher thought processes. She'd smelled sweet and ripe, ready for his possession.

Dakota shook off his wandering thoughts and took a deep breath, allowing the aroma of the ranch and horses to clear his head. He had too much work to accomplish to become so distracted.

The rest of the day flew by in a whirlwind of activity. Although he felt an underlying tension with the cowboys since the mating, the men remained upbeat over their success. The same procedure would take place daily to provide the highest chance of Honey catching while the mare remained in season. Then she would be separated from the other horses during the term of her gestation to avoid injury.

All in all, Dakota was happy with the way things were going. He felt sure the Blacks would be pleased to hear about his progress when they returned from their honeymoon. And Tamara certainly showed signs of being receptive to him, no matter how hard she fought to maintain her distance.

When they all went over to the main house for dinner, the cowboys crowded in close to Tamara, leaving Dakota no choice except sit next to Steph. Neither Riley nor Tamara appeared very happy with this arrangement, yet the meal progressed with lots of happy chatter.

As had become his habit, Dakota assisted with clearing the table after the meal. Because of this, Millie always saved an extra serving of dessert in the kitchen for him. He'd begun to chew a large mouthful of the scrumptious apple pie when Jesse approached him.

"We're headed back to the bunkhouse for a few hands of poker. Care to join us?" he asked with a casual air of indifference.

Although apprehensive of the seeming innocence of the invitation, he accepted. No sooner was Jesse out of earshot before Millie spoke what Dakota was already thinking.

"Watch out for those boys. I can tell they've been plottin'. You'll be lucky to walk away with the shirt still on your back," she said with a chuckle.

Tipping his hat to the older woman, Dakota said, "Yes, ma'am. I know they intend to clean out my wallet." He flashed a wicked grin. "What those boys don't know is that my daddy was a traveling card shark for a time. I just may have a few tricks up my sleeve they've never seen before."

Millie's riotous laughter followed him out of the house. He hadn't seen either Tamara or Steph since dinner. Both women had high-tailed it out of there as soon as the meal was over. It was apparent everyone had sensed the cowboys scheming and chose to get out while the gettin' was good.

By the time he entered the bunkhouse the men were gathered around the scarred wooden table, each with a longneck beer. They had a fresh deck of cards, seal as yet unbroken, ready to go. Taking the last available seat, he nodded to each man. "What's the game?"

With a wide grin displaying a perfect set of white teeth, Jesse responded, "Texas hold 'em."

Well, this was certainly going to be interesting. "Ante and max?"

"Two dollar ante, no single bets over fifty," replied Brock, making eye contact with each of the men in turn to make sure they understood the rules.

"You in?" Riley asked.

After nodding, Dakota schooled his features and settled in for what would most likely be a long night. He accepted the beer handed to him by Zeke, keeping a close watch as Riley broke the seal on the deck of cards and began shuffling. After each of them anted up, Riley dealt the cards and they began to play.

It didn't take long to assess each man's ability, find his weaknesses, and learn his tells. They all had certain verbal or physical cues to give away what cards they were holding. Dakota knew he was being tested and measured. Even though he kept a close eye on the cards, it took three hands to figure out the real game and ferret out how they were cheating.

At first he considered letting it go because their sleight of hand wasn't helping them win anyway, but he wanted the boys to know they were caught. He watched as Jesse slid a card beneath the table, passing it to Brock.

"Must be a good card?"

Everyone grew silent and still. He found their attempt at innocent expressions laughable.

"Might want to get some tarnish remover from the barn for those halos, boys. They're looking a bit...rusty." Unable to hold back any longer, Dakota threw back his head and laughed. "Riley, you gave Jesse an ace during the first hand and Brock passed you two cards in the next round. I do like the little hand signals you're using, although I thought Jesse was picking his nose at one point."

"You're accusing us of cheating?" Zeke questioned. The other guys all stood up slow and easy, making Dakota think of a cheesy old western movie where the cowboys all held their hands over the six-shooters strapped around their hips.

"No. It's not really cheating because you're still losing anyway." Each man gave their meanest scowl, which only served to make Dakota laugh harder. "Come on, guys. You can't fool me. I grew up around world class card players. Forget the games and let's get down to playing some real poker."

He was happily surprised the cowboys took it with good nature and began ribbing each other over how bad they were at cheating. Teasing jaunts like "My grandma plays poker better than you," were grumbled and laughed over. Dakota took the time to teach the men some, not all, of their tells once they settled into the game.

By the end of the evening the others were all moaning and groaning over how he'd managed to bilk them of almost a week's pay each. It'd be a cold day in hell before they invited him to play poker again, Dakota thought, suppressing a chuckle. Still, he was happy with the way things turned out. The other men seemed much more relaxed around him than they had been.

Heading out to check on the horses after the men had called quits to the game, Dakota took in large breaths of the fresh evening air. Being cooped up in the bunkhouse for several hours had left him with a huge need to spend some time outside.

He smiled as he thought about the shocked looks passed among the cowboys with the first hand he'd won. Those looks had turned incredulous as he continued to beat the pants off them with each hand dealt. On occasion, he had let one of the other men win so it didn't look like a total trouncing. He had to leave them some shred of pride.

Leaning against the door to Honey's stall, he rubbed the sweet spot behind the mare's ears, his thoughts focused on the area where he'd set up a private camp in the mountains. Every place he'd ever lived, he always had a special place allowing him escape to be by himself.

Already he had a pretty decent site set up out there in a hidden canyon with a stream running through it. By letting go and allowing his spirit to guide him, Dakota had made his way through the narrow crevice to find an absolute paradise. The valley was surrounded by rocky mountain terrain on all sides, keeping it very secluded.

He was most pleased with the discovery of a natural hot spring. It bubbled up between some rocks at the southernmost end of the area, creating a hot tub of sorts. And a natural crevice in the rock created the perfect sleeping-living area. He had arranged a fire ring for cooking, and even sampled the delicious trout from the stream during his free time when not working.

It was important to him to have a place to go and reconnect with his spirit. There was something about being alone in the wilderness that always brought him closer to the Great Spirit and the four elements—earth, wind, fire, and water. He went into the wilderness to seek truth, answers, renewal, and to learn about himself.

This was part of his heritage he'd learned from his grandparents. Being a "half breed", Dakota had faced a lot of prejudice growing up from white kids in school. Because of this, he had preferred to spend his time in the mountains with his family. The Native American community had been much more accepting of him.

His white father and Indian mother had taught him the best of both worlds. From their example, he learned to judge people by what was in their hearts, spirit and intentions while overlooking the color of their skin.

In the mountains of Colorado, he had learned acceptance, love, and how to maintain a gentle spirit. His education had brought together the best of both cultures, along with old ways and new. Both his parents' families had come together, melding into their own diverse community. He'd attended regular school classes, as well as learning from his combined relations. While he missed being there with his family, Dakota knew his future lay elsewhere. Maybe right here in a different set of mountains on a ranch in Montana.

Thinking about his camp made him itch to head off into those majestic mountains, but now was not the time. He had a responsibility to the Blacks, and to the gentle-spirited horse rubbing her face against his chest.

After checking on each animal, he started back across the yard toward the bunkhouse, yet something pulled him in another direction. Trusting his instincts, Dakota followed the moonlight on a path bringing him behind the main buildings of the ranch. He sensed a troubled, melancholy feeling on the gentle breath of the wind as it teased his unbound hair.

The fierce cry from a bird of prey pierced the night as it sailed from the heavens to snatch up a small field mouse who had dared to run across the clearing. His spirit flew with the bird soaring high into the heavens. He sent a prayer to the Great Spirit on the wings of the courageous, wise creature. Watching the bird helped to settle some of the unease he was feeling.

Dakota sensed the presence of his princess long before seeing her. It only took a moment for him to determine she was the source of the dark emotions he'd read on the wind.

Moving around a copse of fir trees, his breath caught in his throat at the first sight of her. Bathed in the silvery moonlight, she took on an ethereal glow where she sat on the back porch of her cabin in a rocking chair. Her knees were pulled up against her chest, arms hugging her legs close. She had her neck extended, chin resting on the curve of one knee.

She appeared so small and lost. With everything he was, Dakota longed to go to his princess, wrap her in his embrace and provide shelter.

Sheltering her is not the way to help, spoke the ancient voice in his mind. *She must find her connection to the spirit and elemental worlds. While you can set her feet on the path, she must make the journey alone.*

Dakota stood like a ghost among the trees, heart breaking for his spirit mate. The wind stopped blowing and the sharp cry of the eagle again pierced the night. An image of Tamara standing in the canyon, screaming out her overpowering emotions, flashed through his mind. It became clear what he must do, how his plans must be changed. Looking to the heavens, he said a silent thank you.

Tamara needed to heal her spirit and would be able to do so with his help, but not with all the distractions of the ranch. He would have to take her up into the mountains. There she would be able to work through her worldly problems, heal and watch her spirit transcend the hurt and pain keeping her from living a whole life. Then she would be a whole woman, a complete spirit mate.

Getting her there would not be easy, and it would have to wait until he was finished breeding Honey. It would give him a few days to take some more provisions up to the camp and get it ready for his princess.

A burst of excited energy exploded within him, sending his spirit soaring with the wise eagle. This had to work. He wouldn't go much longer before claiming the mate he'd waited so long to find.

"Who's there?" Tamara called out, with a slight squeak to her voice.

Damn! In his excitement, Dakota must have alerted her to his presence. Although he could move across the land as silent as the wind, he now made a point of stepping on a twig and rattling a few branches before revealing himself. "It's just me, princess."

By the time he emerged from behind the trees, Tamara was sitting up with a rigid posture and the lost look long gone from her beautiful face.

"What the hell are you doing skulking around in the dark again, Blackhawk?"

The very sight of her stirred up an animalistic need to bind her to him, to brand her as his own. The fire in her eyes reached out, grabbing hold of his cock, bringing it to life. He needed her with a desperation bordering on pain, but must remain patient.

"Just taking a walk. It's a beautiful night."

A shiver ran through her as Tamara set her bare feet down on the wooden porch floor. The idea of the numerous creatures which might be slithering or scurrying around unseen in the dark was almost enough to drive her back inside the safety of the cabin. With grim determination, she straightened her spine, standing tall as she walked the short distance to where the object of her desire stood.

It bewildered her how she had been sitting there thinking about Dakota and he materialized out of the darkness as though summoned by her mind. Yeah right! She came close to bursting out laughing. Drawing him to her with her thoughts? Now that would be something truly spectacular. She needed him, visualized him, and he appeared. How flippin' convenient.

If only he were able to slake the thirst ravaging her body. What an amazing feat it would be. Since Dakota's arrival at the ranch, she no longer desired the attention of her cowboys. They didn't do it for her anymore. All she wanted now was to capture the attention of the gentle warrior who suddenly held her world balanced in the palm of his capable hand.

Maybe if she were able to get away from him for more than five minutes at a time, she would get over whatever this weird attraction was, but he was always there whenever she turned around. Being on the ranch kept them in close quarters where there was no way to put any distance between them.

She wanted nothing more than to reach out and grab him, try to sate the hungers he stirred within her. Damn, she was so messed up and confused, vacillating between the emotional need for space and the physical needs of her body.

Her physical needs won—hands down. She didn't even want to consider any emotional needs.

When she reached him, Tamara trailed manicured burgundy fingernails down his hard chest. The light contact had bolts of electrical energy surging up her arm and zinging through her from head to toe. Maybe if she got him inside the cabin…

"It's awful late to be out walking around in the dark. Would you like to come inside for a nightcap?"

Dakota's already dark eyes turned pitch black as her fingers continued on their slow path along his torso. When she reached the waistband of his pants, he grabbed her wrist, halting any further movement.

"I don't think that would be the best idea," he ground out. His jaw was clenched tight and a vein pulsed in his forehead. Good, he felt it too.

She thought it was a fabulous idea. Time to turn up the heat.

Bringing on the charm, Tamara leaned into the warmth of his big body, snaking her free hand around his back. Leaning closer, her skin sucked up the heat rolling off him like a sponge. At the feel of his hard erection nestling into her abdomen, she moaned. Tilting her head back, she looked up the long, tantalizing length of him.

God, he looked so damn sexy with his hair loose. She'd wanted to run her fingers through the shiny blue-black locks since the first time she'd run into him. Giving in to the temptation, Tamara wiggled her wrist free and leaned into him for support as she stretched up onto her toes.

"Oh, yes." She actually purred, while threading her fingers through the cool, silky strands. Using her nails, she gave his scalp a massage while letting his soft hair tease the sensitive skin between her fingers.

Dakota's deep moan only served to spur her on. He trailed both hands over her sides and onto her lower back, pulling her even closer against him. By flexing her calves, Tamara rubbed against the glorious length of his erection while trailing her fingers down to his nape. Gazing up at his firm, full lips, she found herself wondering how he would taste. She longed to feel the texture of his lips moving over her own, to delve her tongue into the warm cavern of his mouth.

As if sharing her need, he began to lower his head, maintaining eye contact the whole time. He paused for a moment when their lips were mere inches apart, making her groan in frustration.

Quick to close the distance separating them, Dakota at last brought their lips together in the softest, sweetest kiss Tamara had ever known. With her fingers clasped behind his neck, standing on tiptoes, she struggled to increase the pressure of their kiss.

Moving his hands to her hips, he lifted her closer with little effort, molding their bodies together into one seamless form. Her breasts flattened out against the solid wall of his chest, and his cock settled in against her swollen cunt. Without her even realizing it was happening, she lifted her legs, wrapping them around his lean waist and pressing her heels into his firm ass.

His hands were now free to slide over her subtle curves and cup her ass cheeks, devilish fingers kneading the firm globes as the whole time he ground his cock back and forth against her clit.

Heat poured through her body, sending her blood singing through her veins. Her breasts ached, and cream gushed from the swollen folds of her cunt. Pulling back a bit, she took in great gulps of air. Dakota seemed to be as breathless, but was quick to bring them back together, this time teasing the seam of her lips with his tongue.

Never would she have anticipated such a tender kiss, although gentleness was exactly what she should have expected from such a calm, controlled man. What ensued was a smooth and easy mating of their mouths. Tamara was greedy to drink in his exotic taste, letting her tongue twist and twirl around his and slide over the edge of his teeth. He swallowed each of her small whimpers and moans as the kiss became more heated.

The burning in her oxygen-deprived lungs forced her to pull back, even though she'd not had nearly enough. They were fighting for each breath when he untangled her legs from his waist, letting her make a slow slide over his hard length, teasing her ultra-sensitive nerve endings.

"Go on inside now, princess." He growled the words in a raspy voice reflecting how much their kisses had affected him.

She stood there staring at him in shock. Go inside? Alone? What the fuck?

"You heard me. Get your sweet little ass inside before I do something I'll regret. We'll talk about this later."

Hurt and confusion welled up inside her, and there was no stopping the angry retort. "Don't flatter yourself, stable boy."

She realized what she was doing, but was unable to stop herself from falling into old patterns. Lashing out at Dakota helped to ease the hurtful sting of his rejection.

Turning on her heel, Tamara marched up the porch steps and through the backdoor without once turning to look at him again. In her frustration she slammed the door so hard it sent a jarring vibration through her arm.

"We'll talk about this later," he'd said. Well screw him. He could stand out there and talk to the trees for all she cared because she was not about to discuss what had happened with him.

Chapter Four

Large, dark hands cupped her tender breasts, calloused thumbs teasing turgid nipples. Sinfully wicked sensations streaked straight from the diamond-hard points to pulse along her clit. The big man playing her body like a finely tuned musical instrument was making her hornier than she ever remembered being. Hell, even all four of her cowboys had never managed to get her this worked up.

The musky aroma of feminine arousal permeated the air, increasing her need. Still he stoked her desire higher with each touch, kiss, lick and nip of teeth. Sliding lower down her body, his devilish tongue traced intricate patterns along her tummy, then over her mons after a playful tug on her navel ring. The silky slide of his raven hair against the pale flesh of her legs had her writhing beneath him.

How he managed to bring her to such a state all by himself was beyond her. She had not been able to achieve satisfaction from a single lover in longer than she cared to remember. Each encounter required more stimulation, another partner, a bit more kink for her to gain release. Yet somehow Dakota had her at a fevered pitch all by himself. The man was astounding.

His fingers separated her swollen folds with gentle care, and a heated exhalation caressed her excited clit. She almost came just from the small bit of stimulation. The engorged bundle of nerves pulsed along with the rapid beating of her heart. God, if he would take the sensitive nub between his lips...

The warmth of his tongue traced a slow path from her opening, stopping a fraction below the spot where she most needed his attention.

"Unh..."

"Shh, princess. Just relax."

Relax. Yeah, easy for him to say. The man had her strung tighter than a guitar string, one strum of his thick fingers or wicked tongue over her inflamed clit and she would snap. With shameless abandon, she bucked her needy cunt closer toward his mouth. A bit higher, a little to the left and...

The shrill bleating of the alarm clock brought Tamara flying off the bed.

"Shit!" Spearing her fingers through her hair in frustration, Tamara glared at the offensive instrument. A dream. It had only been a dream. Granted, it was the most intense, body-quaking dream she'd ever experienced, but still only a wet dream. A few minutes longer and she would have gone off like a rocket, soaring into the stratosphere.

Yeah, like that would ever happen. Never in her life had an erotic dream reached fruition. Just like there was no way in hell one man was able to make her as hot as Dakota had in the sleepy imagination. Not only were her panties wet, but her cream coated her thighs. Unbelievable.

She now knew what people meant when they spoke of being "bone weary". After leaving Dakota last night she'd spent endless hours pacing the cabin floor, cussing the annoying Indian. When she'd given in and laid down, sleep had eluded her. Even when she had succumbed to exhaustion, her sleep had been fitful at best. Then the charged erotic dream had filled her mind and increased her restlessness.

Coffee. The wonderful nectar of the gods. It was the only thing capable of getting her through this day. Maybe even an intravenous caffeine infusion was called for.

Ugh, and she had to make it to her bookstore this morning. If she didn't arrive for the nine o'clock meeting with her distributor, Paperback Roundup wouldn't continue to have the hottest new releases.

Her bookstore was Tamara's pride and joy. She had built a thriving business. For the most part it had become self-sufficient. The man she found to manage the store, Wade Garrett, was a godsend who kept the business running with smooth efficiency. Yet there were still certain things she had to...no, *wanted* to handle herself. It also provided a valid excuse to get away.

The need to escape rushed through her. If she got away from the ranch then maybe she'd be able to put a certain Native American cowboy out of her mind. Steph and Jesse would have to start working harder on getting the store's website up and running. Their work together was the primary thing keeping her on the ranch right now, other than her friendship with Van. Once that project was done, she wouldn't have to be around so much.

For some reason the thought of not being on the ranch created an ache in her chest. Tamara decided it was too early in the morning to analyze the reaction. Definitely not something to face before consuming a large quantity of caffeine.

Setting the coffeemaker to work its magic in the kitchen, she headed into the bathroom for a quick shower. The way she'd woken up should have been enough of a warning it was going to be a crappy day, but the hits kept on coming.

With her eyes clamped shut against the stream of water she'd grabbed the wrong bottle from the ledge in the shower stall and ended up pouring body wash onto her hair. In her rush to finish and beat the clock, she ended up nicking her skin twice with a dull razor. Damn, the water burned when it hit the shallow cuts. The blouse she had wanted to wear had a stain right in the center of her left breast, and she ended up trying on four different outfits before settling on something acceptable.

Although she found it odd not to smell the coffee brewing, Tamara didn't give the situation a whole lot of thought until she walked into the kitchen. Somehow she had managed not to close the basket containing the grounds all the way, so all she had was a big mess on the kitchen counter.

Things continued to go down hill when she returned to the bathroom. The hairdryer died with a brilliant shower of sparks and a puff of smoke as she switched the infernal device on. If she had any sense, she would crawl back under the covers and hide for the rest of the day.

She stared at the tired person reflected in the mirror, noting the many signs of her age revealed in the image. Small crow's feet sprouted from the corners of her eyes, and thin lines had formed next to her mouth, marking the passage of time and a hard life. She ignored the evidence and went about the motions of getting ready to face her lousy karma head on.

The last straw came as she was putting on her makeup. One of her cowboys tapped on the bathroom window as he passed the cabin, startling her into smearing mascara into her eye and in a black streak down her face. When she figured out which moron had caused the incident to happen, he was a dead man. Riley, the ultimate clown, was the most likely suspect. Tamara pictured the wide, shit-eating grin splitting his fool face when she'd started cussing again.

In a fit of frustration she stormed from the cabin toward the main house to use Savannah's hairdryer. She knew she must look a mess, hair hanging in a wet mass around her face, the top half of her shirt damp from absorbing the moisture dripping from her hair. Black streaks of makeup down the left side of her face. Yet as she stalked across the yard, hands balled into tight fists at her sides, one of those ornery cowboys had the nerve to whistle.

Slamming the front door behind her, Tamara stalked through the kitchen where Millie and Steph sat sipping coffee. Neither woman said a word as she slammed around the large space getting a mug and creamer, then filling the cup. She only paused for a moment to take a tentative sip of the hot brew before heading straight for the staircase.

"Who lit the fuse on her tampon?" Steph joked when Tamara was halfway up the staircase.

"I heard that," she growled over her shoulder, never missing a step. On a normal day she would laugh at such a witty jibe, but not in the mood she found herself in. And there was one person to blame for her crappy morning—Dakota Blackhawk.

Heads up, horseman. Payback's a bitch!

CR80

He'd been standing in the ranch yard earlier when Tamara stalked over to the house before heading out in her Jeep. Dakota had been surprised by the disheveled state of his princess. It was blatantly obvious from her rigid stance and balled up fists her morning had not been going well.

As she'd stalked across the yard, Riley, idiot that he was, whistled at the hell cat. Dakota wanted to smack the fool across the back of his head. Whistling at the pissed-off princess was not the smartest thing the man had ever done. Of course, the other man was well known for his harebrained ideas and schemes.

From what he'd heard since arriving at the ranch, Dakota knew Savannah and Riley fed off each others' wild ideas, often leading to crazy stunts. Not that long ago, Brock had come close to dying while playing one of their crazy games. From listening to Millie and Steph, he'd learned things had settled down for a while after the near miss, but he didn't think it would last much longer. The cowboys were restless and fidgety. Between Tamara no longer turning to them and the long summer days of hard work, those boys were ready to blow off some steam.

As the day wore on it didn't surprise Dakota to find himself alone in the eerie quiet of the ranch yard. Steph even sensed something going on and wandered outside to take a break from her website design work.

"Where is everyone?" she asked, standing back slightly from where he bathed one of the horses.

"Hey, Steph. I think they're working up one of their elaborate stunts. It's been too quiet around here this afternoon."

They stood chatting, once in a while hearing an odd clanking noise from the barn, when Steph brought up the subject weighing on her mind.

"What was wrong with Tamara this morning? She was so out of sorts. Is she angry with the boys or is it something you did?"

Steph was certainly perceptive. Hmm...how to explain what Tamara was going through to the sweet, innocent young woman. He was sure she had no experiences which would relate to the inner turmoil his princess was struggling with.

"Tamara is a complicated woman. She's going through some changes in her life and fighting it every step of the way.

She won't find happiness until she's able to let go of the past and come to terms with her pain."

The banging and clanking noises in the barn continued to increase as they stood talking. He'd noticed the cowboys disappearing into the barn every afternoon when their chores were finished, and before long the sounds of something being built would begin. They would come and go carrying the oddest items. What they were up to was beyond him. Dakota hoped their activities would ease the mounting tension.

"The boys are so strung out since she has been ignoring them. I hope she can get things sorted out soon. I'm tired of walking on eggshells around here." Dakota agreed with Steph's assessment of the situation. Nobody would relax until the pressure built to a head and released.

As was typical with the way things seemed to go on the Shooting Star ranch, all hell broke loose at once. Dakota and Steph stood watching as the cowboys dragged strange, mixed-up creations from the barn and up the nearby hill. From the looks of things, they had each crafted some form of a soapbox racer out of whatever discarded clutter they'd found lying around the ranch.

"Now this should be interesting," Dakota remarked. After returning the horse to its stall, he took Steph by the arm, leading her out of the potential path of the ragtag vehicles. "Let's find a safe spot to watch the follies."

The most out-of-the-way place to sit and still be able to see what was going on turned out to be the front porch of Tamara's cabin. Steph went inside and got them both a tall, cold glass of sweet tea. They sat together on the porch swing to watch the show.

The first up were Riley and Zeke. As they climbed into their carts, Dakota was glad to see them exchange their Stetsons for helmets. Brock and Jesse stood behind the carts, ready to give them a shove off. After a quick countdown the two men came barreling down the hill, their excited hoots and hollers not to be outdone by the clanking and clattering sounds of the haphazard carts.

As spectators, Dakota and Steph found it impossible not to cheer them on, laughing loud and boisterous when Riley's cart rolled over on its side and continued to slide down the hill. The comedy show continued when the men switched places. As Jesse and Brock rocketed down the hill, Jesse tried bumping his friend's cart off the course. By the time they reached the bottom, both carts had acquired several dings and scrapes from the rough and rowdy ride.

At one point, Zeke's cart lost a wheel and had to be taken back to the barn for repairs, but when the front bumper hung off Brock's cart, he simply pulled it the rest of the way off and tossed it to the side. The competition became heated, narrowing down to a tie-breaker between Riley and Jesse.

Mandy had come out of the main house, and was sitting on the porch watching the festivities. Every once in a while she would jump up to cheer for one of the men.

Steph had gotten into the action. Standing at the bottom of the hill with Riley's hat, she started each race. The woman would hold the hat up high over her head then lowering it with dramatic flair, run back to the safety of the porch. As she flew up the steps with laughter trailing behind her, Steph launched herself into the rocker. Dakota caught her with ease, lowering Steph to the seat beside him.

The fun continued until Tamara's charcoal gray Jeep came tearing up the road. As she parked in front of the cabin, Dakota caught a glimpse of the murderous look on her face right before he heard Brock's shouted warning.

"Look out! He's gonna crash!"

Looking up the hill he saw both front wheels had torn away from Jesse's cart, and the man had lost the ability to steer the fast moving projectile, which was headed straight for the Jeep.

Dakota vaulted over the porch railing as Tamara jumped from the vehicle in a blind rage, muttering and cussing, never noticing the out-of-control cart headed her way. He felt his left hip pop, and knew there was no way he would reach Tamara in time to get her out of harm's way. Blinding pain shot through his pelvis and down his entire leg as he ran, but he would not stand there and watch his spirit mate be run down. Somehow he had to protect her.

The weakness was a sore spot, a point of contention, for Dakota. Each step he took seemed to drag on forever, like he tried to run through waist deep snow. It was one of those moments when everything took on a slow motion quality. Like in those dreams where no matter how fast you run, you can barely get one foot in front of the other and make no progress. The landscape becomes endless, the point you need to reach seeming farther and farther away.

A quick glance over his shoulder confirmed the hurtling cart's treacherous path. Stephanie's shrill scream sliced across the yard as Dakota stumbled once, then struggled to pull himself upright.

Jesse's shouts of warning went unheeded by the wildcat as she stood ignoring the entire scene unfolding before her, too wrapped up in jealous rage to see through the emotions.

With a burst of speed he wouldn't have thought possible of the young woman, Steph charged past him, hitting Tamara in the abdomen with her shoulder like a professional football linebacker. The two women crashed into the side of the Jeep, landing on the ground in a tangled mass as Dakota's leg gave out and he fell face first into the dirt.

He looked up in time to see the cart barrel over the exact spot where Tamara had stood, then crash into the corner of the porch, spilling its passenger out unharmed. As he dropped his head back down, Dakota heard Tamara ranting and raving at the other woman for attacking her, not yet having realized Steph had saved her life.

Somehow, Steph managed to escape the other woman's flailing arms and made it to his side where he lay, writhing in pain. She was the only one, other than the ranch owners, who knew of his injuries.

"How bad is it?" she questioned, laying a gentle, comforting hand on his arm.

Dakota couldn't speak. His jaw was held clenched tight against the pain of what felt like a searing-hot poker had taken the place of his leg. As the others gathered around, Steph explained about his synthetic hip. Snatching Tamara's purse out of her hands, Steph pulled out the cell phone, ready to call for an ambulance.

His "no" was not much above a raspy whisper. Clearing his throat, Dakota tried again. "No. No ambulance. It's just dislocated."

Brock was the first one to react. "Tell us what to do." His voice held calm authority, helping center the others.

Noticing Mandy standing off to the side of the group, he gave the girl a strained smile. There was no way he wanted her to watch this. "Someone take Mandy inside first."

Once the girl was gone it took several minutes for him to grit out between his clenched teeth what would need to be done to put his hip back in the socket. Hell, he was an expert at the process. This was the third dislocation since his injury.

Tamara sat in the dirt, cradling his head in her lap. If he weren't in so much pain, he would've enjoyed the position. In his current state, he took what comfort he was able to gain from her trembling hand stroking through his hair.

Zeke brought out the first aid kit and injected a pain medication into the opposite hip, then rolled him onto his right side. They waited a few minutes for the medication to begin taking effect before Brock and Jesse moved into place, one man at his knee, the other at his hip. Folding a leather work glove, Dakota put it between his teeth then nodded to signal his readiness. Steph sat before him, nervously squeezing his hands.

Jesse squatted, straddling Dakota's leg, wrapping both arms around his thigh above the knee. Brock bent his right knee, placing his lower leg over Dakota's hip. The small amount of pressure had Dakota biting into the glove to keep from screaming.

In a coordinated effort, Jesse pulled his leg down while Brock used his body weight to press the hip back into the socket. Dakota felt the tug of Tamara's hands as they fisted in his hair when he hollered and bit down on the glove. The loud pop of his hip snapping back into place made the two women startle, but allowed him to take a gasping breath past the glove for the first time in countless minutes.

He was afraid he'd hurt Steph's hands when he'd squeezed down on them. Tears and dirt streaked her sweet face. He looked up into shocked eyes turned a stunning shade of gray. With a gentle squeeze, he pried his fingers from between hers, and removed the glove from his mouth, taking great gulping breaths of air.

Immense, wracking sobs shook Tamara's delicate frame, bouncing his head still resting in her lap. With careful movements he rolled onto his back then hooked a hand behind her neck, pulling her face down to his.

"It's okay now, princess," he breathed against her mouth before capturing her lips with his own. The chaste kiss offered reassurance she needed.

The other men began to joke and tease, relieved the tension had been lifted. Dakota shook his head upon hearing Riley's quip. "Damn, never thought about hurting myself to catch the ladies' attention."

The others all laughed along and teased as their kiss turned into a frantic affirmation of well-being. Tamara was slow to pull back, panting for breath, running her fingers all over his face in the most heart-wrenching, tender caress.

Trying to help relieve the tension, Dakota teased, "All right, boys, mind your manners and help the old man up."

Without hesitation, four hands appeared before him, ready to offer assistance. Dakota grabbed hold of two of those helping hands, and was pulled up with care, while the other two men came in close to his sides to provide support.

Tamara was on her feet standing before him quicker than the blink of an eye, issuing orders. "Be careful with him, you buffoons. Take him into the cabin. There's no way he can make it to the bunkhouse."

Although he felt like he could make it, Dakota wasn't about to disagree. Nodding his assent, he leaned on the other men as they helped him up the steps and straight to Tamara's bed. After laying him back, Steph questioned if he needed anything before chasing the cowboys out of the cabin, leaving Tamara and him alone.

He listened in silence for several minutes as she fumbled around in the bathroom, cussing and berating herself as a fool. She came and sat down next to him on the bed, wiping the dirt from his face with a cool cloth. Looking into her bright green eyes he clearly saw the love and tenderness she fought against tooth and nail.

Capturing her hand, Dakota stilled her movements. "It's okay, Tamara. I've been through this before with my hip. I'll be fine." Her gaze met his, and he was struck speechless by the strong, unguarded emotions revealed in the depths of her eyes.

He patted the side of the bed. "Please, sit down. I want to tell you what happened."

She sat where he'd indicated and Dakota began talking. It wasn't a pretty story or one he enjoyed telling, but he wanted her to know.

"I didn't start out breeding and training horses. I started as a competitive rider. The U.S. equestrian team selected me to compete in the 2004 Summer Olympics in Athens."

"What an honor!"

He nodded. "Yes, it was a wonderful honor and an incredible opportunity. Too bad I had to mess it up."

It was during the second day, on the grueling cross-country course, the two of them went down. The event was designed to test speed, endurance, and ability of horse and rider to jump over obstacles, as well as the rider's knowledge of pace and use of the horse's abilities. This was not an event to be undertaken when physically or mentally impaired.

"My coach tried to convince me to withdraw since my head wasn't in it, but I was too stubborn." He sighed. "My grandmother had died while we traveled to Greece, and I was grieving."

"I'm so sorry for your loss." Tamara ran her fingers over his cheek.

"Thank you, princess."

A strong sense of discipline, work ethic, and a responsibility to the rest of his team had driven him. Even knowing it was dangerous to compete, he would not let everyone down, including himself. He'd carried on in honor of his grandmother.

"We were three-quarters of the way through the fifty-seven-hundred-meter distance with fifteen jumps left to go. The most difficult hidden jump took us by surprise, despite having walked the course several times and knowing it well."

They'd gone down hard, landing in a confused mass of man and horse—arms, legs and hooves. Dakota was to blame. The accident was the direct result of his lack of concentration.

"My left hip was shattered, requiring four surgeries to put it back together in a workable fashion. Hunter faired somewhat better, managing only to pull tendons and muscles in an effort to right himself. Neither of us was able to compete anymore. It's the reason why the idea of getting in on the ground floor of the Shooting Star's equestrian program was so appealing. This is my chance to still work with horses who may one day win competitions."

Savannah already assured him she would be turning the horses over to his capable care. It was a chance he never imagined being offered. One of the important deciding factors had been his horse. The Blacks were enthusiastic and supportive about having Hunter at the ranch to continue rehabilitating from his injuries. They'd assured Dakota he would be permitted whatever time necessary to work with his own horse.

He understood the ranch was expanding at a rapid rate, and the owners were working toward being general overseers. Their intention was for the different working areas of the ranch to be run by a hand-picked staff of pros. This idea suited Dakota very well.

"The Blacks agreed not to tell anyone because I didn't want my abilities questioned or to be treated with kid gloves."

"I can see why you kept it a secret. The boys would've used it to tease and harass you."

Of course, she of all people understood. He knew Tamara kept her own secrets, hiding her true self from her friends. Dakota hoped she'd learn to trust him enough at some point to let him see her beautiful spirit shine instead of hiding behind the attitude. At least he felt better for having shared his story. Now if he could manage to keep her close...

"The medicine is making me tired. How about helping me take off my boots before I fall asleep."

With a nod, Tamara set about her task, being very careful of his left leg. After removing his socks she pulled a lightweight blanket over him, and turned to move away.

"Princess," he whispered, waiting for her to turn back. When she did he took her hand, pulling her to his side. "Stay with me."

Again she nodded then crawled onto the bed, snuggling up against his right side. The last thought to filter through his drug-hazed brain was how good it felt to have her lying there, right where she belonged.

CRSO

Damn, just what he'd expected, waking up alone in her bed. Although he'd hoped she'd still be lying next to him, Dakota was a realistic man. By now, Tamara was running scared from the emotions stirred up by the day's events. It was time to take drastic measures before she shut down again.

Soreness shot through his left hip and leg when he stood. Dakota winced, but was undeterred by the flash of searing pain. To succeed in what he had planned would require swift, decisive maneuvering. Everything was in place at his spirit camp. He'd spent all his free time in the evenings making sure it was. Now all he had to do was capture one gun-shy, wild filly and get her there. The rest would take care of itself.

Not bothering with his boots, Dakota gathered up his things and headed for the bunkhouse. A hot shower would help loosen his muscles and relieve the burning ache. Afterward, a deep rub with one of his special herbal creams and he'd be good to go. The long ride ahead was going to be difficult, but he'd been through worse. Helping Tamara was worth the discomfort.

Thoughts about all the surgeries to repair his shattered hip, followed by countless hours of physical therapy, made him shudder. Having survived the medical torture, he knew he'd survive anything life threw his way.

Dakota was thankful everyone was most likely at dinner and the bunkhouse was empty. The last thing he wanted to do right now was answer a bunch of questions. Although none of the men had a strong emotional attachment with Tamara, they would still fight to protect her if they felt she needed them. Facing down four riled cowboys was not in his plan. Not yet.

After showering, he changed into a worn pair of jeans, clean shirt and soft moccasins. The brief note he left on the table told them he was taking some time off to rest his hip, giving no indication of where he was going or when he'd be back. No one would even expect a note from Tamara. It was not out of character for her to take off for a few days at a time on a whim without telling anyone, according to what he'd gleaned from the others.

Hunter called out an equine greeting before Dakota had even made it through the stable door. He greeted the big horse with the brush of a hand down Hunter's long face and soft muzzle. The sight of the big, mixed-up looking horse always lightened his heart. As was typical of the Leopard variety of Spotted Appaloosa, Hunter looked like he'd been splattered with brown and white paint. Each member of the breed had its own, individual color pattern as distinctive as a fingerprint. Hunter's primary color was a snowy white decorated with splashes of reddish brown, most of which were concentrated on his face and neck but also in a sporadic spread across his powerful body.

After saddling and bridling Hunter, he picked out a calm palomino mare for Tamara and repeated the process. He strapped on the saddle bags he'd prepared and the only thing remaining to be done was to capture his princess. He decided to wait until he was certain the cowboys would all be in the bunkhouse and use the cover of darkness to aid in spiriting her away.

Chapter Five

Walking across the ranch yard to her cabin, Tamara wondered if Dakota would still be in her bed. What happened earlier had left her feeling like a bundle of exposed nerves. She really needed some time to get her head back on straight. Emotions she didn't know how to handle were hammering at her from all sides and she felt downright battered.

One side of her prayed he would still be there, waiting for her to care for him. The other side, the scarred side, would be happy to find her cabin empty as usual. Empty was safer, right? She didn't know how she would handle the injured man lying in her bed since she had no experience with taking care of anyone. Hell, she had enough trouble taking care of herself. She wasn't a nurse maid and had no idea how to approach the task.

Maybe she should take him a tray of food or see if he needed some more of the pain medication Zeke had given her after dinner. The meal had been an unusual, somber affair, with the typically playful cowboys being quiet, watchful and expectant. Everyone seemed to be waiting for her to say or do something.

Well, she wasn't about to be their evening's entertainment. Let them think whatever they wanted. It didn't matter much one way or the other. She hadn't interacted with the boys to any great extent since before the wedding, and had no plans to do so anytime soon. They'd have to figure things out for themselves.

While she did miss their sexual escapades, Tamara knew that part of their friendship was over. Something inside her had changed and playing with the cowboys no longer held the appeal it once had. Hell, half the fun had always been the danger of discovery and the shock factor involved. Since Van had walked in on them, everyone knew about their bunkhouse games and the thrill was gone.

She refused to let the timing of this sudden change penetrate her consciousness. It was a mere coincidence Dakota's arrival coincided with the timing of this big change in her. On some deep level, Tamara knew she was deluding herself, yet she was unwilling to admit to her false beliefs, happy to live in her fantasy world for the time being. Life was easier to handle with her denial firmly in place.

Complete and utter silence hit her the moment she stepped into the cabin. It had a deserted feeling. Squashing down the hope and anticipation she'd harbored at the thought of taking care of Dakota, she moved through the familiar space and into the bedroom. Her heart dropped down into her stomach when she saw the empty bed. The only sign marking his presence was the rumpled section of the bed linens.

The walls started to close in as the crushing weight of solitude slammed into her small body. Granted, she did not like to spend much time by herself, but she'd never felt this bothered by silence before. She didn't remember a time in her life when she had felt quite so alone.

Rejected.

The word bounced around in her mind, echoing over and over again in the silence. She didn't know how or why he'd left, but he had, not trusting her to take care of him.

Fuck! She was thrust back in time with cruel abruptness, back to the ultimate rejection. The painful memory of being six, standing before the social services worker as the woman spoke like she wasn't even there and didn't matter. She'd stood there—face streaked with dirt and tears, thumb in her mouth—as the cold woman had nonchalantly talked about the fact no one wanted Tamara. Not her drug-addicted mother or her absentee father. All she'd had in the world was the raggedy cloth doll tucked in a tight hold under one arm.

Her mind began to drift through the multitude of loveless foster families she'd been thrust upon who only wanted her for one reason—the check they would receive each month from the state. Every grubby male hand that had ever tried to take something from her flashed through her mind within a matter of seconds. Every hollered threat and demeaning task she'd been required to complete sliced through her head like a knife, leaving behind a sharp pain.

At first, she had been happy to go along with anything, hoping these caretakers would love her...maybe just a bit. It had fast become apparent no matter what she did, no matter how hard she tried, she was unlovable.

As she'd aged and physically matured, the foster mothers would only put up with her until they discovered the attentions she received from her foster fathers. Then she would once again be forced to pack up her small suitcase of mismatched clothing and get dumped on another family.

If the family had children of their own things were much worse. The children were always cruel. They would set her up for trouble then laugh while she was spanked or locked away in a room or closet. She'd been stunned at the lengths kids would go in order to maintain their status in their families.

With a mental slap, Tamara pulled herself from the painful memories. In his understanding way and calm presence, Dakota had managed to strip away part of the thick shields she'd built around herself, leaving her exposed to excruciating, painful emotions she was not equipped to handle. Then he had left. Somehow his rejection was far worse than any she'd ever gone through before.

Well, fuck him. Who needs the bastard, anyway? Not me, that's for sure! The angry thoughts rang hollow in her mind.

Slamming the bedroom door with a deafening crash behind her, Tamara stomped into the living room where she cranked up her small stereo system as loud as it would go. If anything had the ability to drown out the painful echoes of her anguished past in her head it was some loud, boot-stomping country music.

Banging around in the kitchen, she cut two large limes into wedges, setting the bowl down with a pronounced thunk on the small dining table. She grabbed a shot glass from one cabinet, along with a brand new bottle of Jose Cuervo tequila. Plopping down into an old chair, she cracked the seal with a firm twist of her wrist.

Never before did she remember being quite so pissed off. The son-of-a-bitch thought he'd stir up her emotions then leave her in the lurch. Well, she would tell him a thing or two. Right after she fortified herself with some liquid courage. Hell, maybe she'd drink thoughts of him right out of her mind and the desire for him right out of her body.

Yeah, right!

She was proud to notice only a slight shake in her hand as she poured the golden liquid into the glass. The anger raging through her blood stream made her feel super strong. For the briefest moment, she wondered if it were possible to break the thick shot glass in her punishing grip.

After licking a wet path across the fleshy pad between the base of her thumb and knuckle of her first finger, Tamara sprinkled a liberal coating of salt over the damp skin. She sucked off the salt, getting a slight jolt from the sensation it created. Picking up the glass, she raised it to her lips, tossed back her head, and let the fiery liquid sear a burning path down her throat.

Immediate fingers of heat, accompanied by a tingling sensation, spread out from her chest and abdomen. *Hell yeah!* A good buzz was exactly what she needed. Popping a wedge of lime into her mouth, Tamara sucked hard on the bitter fruit, cutting some of the burn created by the alcohol.

Shot after shot, she repeated the process, singing along with the music blasting through her brain and shaking the little cabin. With each drink she became number to the burn of the tequila, more immune to the sting of Dakota's rejection. The more she drank, the less her anger drove her to confront him, coming to the decision it was par for the course and didn't matter.

With each shot, she toasted the bastard for his effective manner of stopping her from making a total fool out of herself. What the hell had made her think someone like Dakota Blackhawk cared about her, or that she gave a shit about him? The very idea was total lunacy. She was unlovable and had nothing to give to someone like him.

Someone pounded on the cabin door at one point, but she ignored the intrusion until whoever it was gave up and went away. Tamara lost track of how many shots she'd thrown back as she sang at the top of her lungs to the rowdy music. The last thing she remembered was cussing a certain man, and thinking about how fucked up it was that he was an Indian who liked to play cowboy. The whole thing was completely ass backwards if you asked her.

Too bad he didn't want to play Cowgirl and Indian, or even Capture the Cowgirl with her. Either game would have been interesting.

When her head got too heavy for her neck to hold up, she let it drop to the table. Her bleary eyes shut and she slipped into a drunken, dead-to-the-world state of sleep.

CRSO

He moved through the inky black night without creating even the slightest whisper of sound. The soft moccasins on his feet allowed him to move with the light-footed grace of a deer, his eyes not requiring much light to see the way. The silver rays cast by the small sliver of moon high in the sky cloaked him in darkness, while at the same time lighting his way.

Earlier, Dakota had sat in a meditative state, drinking in the sounds of the ranch until long after everyone had turned in for the night. The only noises to disturb the peaceful night now were those created by nocturnal creatures, and the pounding music, which continued to pour from the cabin.

His emotions had become conflicted while watching Brock approach the cabin and pound on the door for several long minutes. He was angry with the man for attempting to go to his princess, yet he was also grateful to witness the concern etched into the serious man's features.

Leading the two horses to the back porch, Dakota dropped the reins, knowing both animals would stay close to where he'd left them. His hip ached as he climbed the stairs, but he would not let the minor inconvenience keep him from his plans.

Healing his spirit mate was too important to be distracted by his own physical weakness.

Popping the simple lock on the back door was easy. Once inside, he moved in silence through the small space. When he reached the stereo, Dakota considered leaving the music playing, but dismissed the idea. If the music were still blaring in the morning it would draw attention and someone would come to investigate.

It took several moments for his hearing to return to normal after the abrupt cease to the excruciating, deafening noise. He almost sensed the entire ranch letting out a deep breath with the precipitous return to the normal peace and quiet.

Finding Tamara passed out at the kitchen table was not what he'd expected. Seeing his princess in such a state created an incredible pain within his heart. Had he not been convinced he was taking the right path with her before, he was now. She was in desperate need of his intervention. Tamara needed to spend some time with herself facing down the fears, anger and hurt she battled against daily, no matter how hard she would fight against doing so.

He spent a few minutes making it appear to the casual observer like she'd gone away on one of her spur of the moment trips. In the bedroom, he packed casual clothes along with the sturdiest-looking pair of boots she had. In the bathroom, her tooth and hair brushes were added to the saddle bag then everything was loaded onto the palomino. He attached the mare's reins to the back of Hunter's saddle, knowing she would follow along without complaint.

The more he thought about it, Dakota decided Tamara being passed out was a blessing. This way she wouldn't see where they were going, and therefore wouldn't know how to find her way back to the ranch. He'd also be in for a lot less of a struggle with her in her current condition. Yes, this would all work well into his plans.

Now, to get them both settled onto Hunter's saddle. With one arm below her knees and the other supporting her back, Dakota lifted his princess into his embrace with relative ease. She felt so slight and fragile in his arms, putting barely any additional strain on his hip.

He had to laugh at the idea of her being anything but strong. Tamara would never consider herself to be fragile. He was pretty certain she thought of herself as a fearsome fighter.

Getting the two of them settled onto Hunter's broad back turned out to be easier than he'd anticipated. The porch put him at the perfect height to hoist his good leg over the saddle and sit right down. The soft creaking of his leather saddle was the only sound to disturb the quiet night.

Tamara stirred for a moment in his arms as he positioned her sideways across his lap, head resting against his chest. Speaking in a soothing monotone, Dakota whispered ancient words of comfort as they headed out into the night.

In her drunken sleep, Tamara snuggled close into the shelter of his body. Each gentle movement Hunter made created a friction between the curve of her hip and his now aching cock. No matter how he tried to position her, there was no way to prevent the sensual brush of her body against his.

The way she curled into his arms as she lay across his lap, fisting her small hand in his shirt, made his heart sing. In repose, her relaxed face appeared both young and angelic with her dark lashes fanned over flushed cheeks. He had no trouble picturing her as a beautiful child with pink cheeks, wearing her hair in pigtails.

It hurt him to think of all she had been through. He wished he'd been there to fight the battles with her, yet those very trials had made her the person he loved. And once her heart was healed, his princess would be a spirited mate able to weather any storm to cross their paths—a true life partner.

Dakota was quick to realize whenever he stopped talking to her, Tamara became restless, while with each word flowing from his lips, she settled into his embrace. It seemed her heart already knew him well. The realization sent his spirit soaring.

Looping the reins around the saddle horn, Dakota guided Hunter using only the slight pressure from his legs. He kept his left arm behind Tamara's back, providing support. The fingers of his other hand traced every detail of her sweet face. He committed every angle, curve and line to memory. Had he been blessed with the ability to paint, he knew he'd be able to create an accurate portrait of her from the memories he was burning into his very soul.

As his fingers trailed a gentle path across her cheek, she turned toward his hand, attempting to maintain the soothing contact. She wiggled in his arms, pressing the soft, rounded curve of her hip against his erection with a firm pressure. Dakota groaned and settled himself in for what would be an excruciating ride.

Throughout their trek, he spoke to her, detailing his vision of their entwined lives. He allowed his fingers the liberty of tracing the delicate column of her neck, the sharp angle of her collarbone beneath the thin material of the shirt she wore, the fine muscles along her arms. He longed to release the inner beauty, which he knew would outshine even her exquisite outer loveliness. When she opened herself up to embrace life, he had no doubt she would outshine the sun.

Tamara whimpered as his fingers traced the soft skin along the inside of her arm. Feeling quite the cad for doing so, Dakota was unable to resist exploring each gentle curve, hollow and graceful line of her lithe body. This woman was his very heart, his life, his spirit. He was determined to know every delectable inch of her.

His left arm lay curved behind her back, his hand resting over her hip in an awkward position. He allowed his hand to slide upward, palm cupping her firm breast. Even in her drunken sleep, she arched and rotated into his touch, pressing the small globe into his hand. When he felt her nipple begin to rise, Dakota teased the elongated nub between his thumb and finger.

His right hand was as busy learning the curves of her smooth legs. As his fingers neared the juncture of her thighs, his princess grabbed hold of his hand, pressing his palm against her pussy. Her hips bucked in an instinctive move as his hand stroked over her heated mound.

The scent of her arousal hit him like a physical blow, causing his aching cock to swell even further. He was amazed this was happening, and with her in a drunken stupor.

No. He was not going to take advantage of her.

With the intention of stopping before anything got started, Dakota tried to pull his hand away, but the wildcat grabbed his wrist with her other hand, fighting to hold him in place, moaning and whimpering while she rode his palm. The thin material of her shorts was not much of a barrier, and her intense heat filled his palm.

He didn't have the willpower to fight this. She was so damn sexy he gave in, following her lead as she pulled on his wrist, guiding his fingers under the edge of her shorts and panties. He felt her breast swelling against his other hand as he tweaked her nipple. Her entire body became animated by sinuous motion as his hand inched closer and closer to her moist heat.

Questing fingers sliding over smooth, naked skin sent a jolt of heat surging through his blood stream. His fingers caressed every slick inch of her bare slit before parting wet, swollen folds. Tamara arched even higher into his palm as he brushed against her clitoris.

He was history. There was no way he'd stop now. Each breathless pant, moan and whimper drove him wild with the need to see her come apart in his arms. Hot cream soaked his fingers as he slid two of them into the tight clasp of her drenched pussy, pumping in and out, curving the tips to tease along her sweet spot. The heel of his hand stroked her clit with each movement. Each gasp and whimper from her pouty lips only served to increase his fervor.

Once his fingers were buried deep within her pussy, held in place by the tight squeeze of her thighs, his princess did the most unexpected thing. With both her hands now free, she reached out in an awkward attempt to unbutton his jeans. When she managed to slide down the zipper, the minx caught his cock in her hand as it sprang free. Her fingers felt like heaven wrapped around his hard shaft.

The positioning was cramped, and being on horseback made things difficult, but he wouldn't let this chance to experience her touch pass him by. He shifted their bodies to make more room then settled back to enjoy the ride.

Dakota couldn't take his eyes from the blissful expression on her sweet face as she pumped his shaft in the same rhythm he fingered her pussy. He burned the look into his mind—let it become imprinted on his very spirit. His greatest desire was to bring the magnificent look to her face as often as possible for the rest of their days.

As her orgasm drew near, Tamara pumped her fist faster, bucking her hips with wild abandon against his hand. The slick walls of her pussy clamped down like a warm vise on his fingers right before she began to convulse. But the most incredible pleasure was yet to be experienced.

At the moment she gave her body over to him, she threw back her head and cried out his name. Never had he heard such a sweet sound. His spirit soared high into the night sky as sizzling heat surged through his cock, hot streams of his seed arching over his abdomen as he transcended place and time, flying among the stars with the Great Spirit, greeting the legendary hunters of the past.

Her movements slowed then settled as they came back down to earth. Dakota reveled in the experience. He'd heard stories of the incredible heights spirit mates took each other to, but never imagined anything quite as wondrous as what he'd shared with his princess.

Now more than ever their path became crystal clear within his mind while his spirit basked in the glow of bonding with its true mate. There was no way he'd ever let her go. No matter how much she fought against their bond there was nothing she'd be able to do to push him away.

Chapter Six

The weirdest disjointed visions poured through her mind, along with a piercing emotional sting. On some level, Tamara knew she was in a strange, dreamlike state, but was unable to direct the flow of the bizarre phenomenon as she was sometimes able to do with dreams. She also tried to wake up, but no matter how hard she tried all she could do was hang on for the ride.

Her life was laid out before her like an intricately woven fabric. Several gaping holes in the cloth marred the beauty, and she was certain the holes were the traumas which had shaped the person she'd become. With wisdom born from life's experience, Tamara knew these were the very things that must be mended if she were ever to be happy and whole. To find where she belonged, she must repair the tapestry.

The vision shifted and she saw the pieces of a puzzle fitting into place to form a complete picture. The piece representing her hadn't been lost at all, but instead fit perfectly with all the others. She knew if it were removed there would be a glaring hole in its place.

What she saw appeared to be enchanting and complete, but she was unable to get a clear glimpse of exactly what it was. Maybe it wasn't time yet for her to see the whole picture. At least there was a space for her in the image, which stirred very unfamiliar feelings of belonging and relief she wasn't sure how to deal with.

Typically, Tamara saw a younger, curvier version of herself in her dreams. This was the first dream she ever remembered seeing herself the way she actually was. The woman she looked upon was too thin, showing the signs of rough wear and tear. The results of a hard life lived on the edge. Seeing herself as she appeared to the real world told her the visions were significant. Maybe portentous of something major happening. Or maybe she was simply losing it.

Next she was in a room with several twin-sized beds. A tall, dark-haired guy she'd lusted after in the tenth grade was there with her. They were working in a companionable silence, making up the beds. For some reason she didn't recall his name. While it had been very important to her at one time, it seemed irrelevant now.

The vision changed again and she was lying on her side on one of the beds watching TV. The guy was behind her, head propped up on one bent arm to see over top of her shoulders. They weren't touching in any way, just lying there watching images flicker across the screen.

The guy shifted his position and she felt the light pressure of his leg against hers. Tamara didn't pull away, presuming it to be an innocent touch, but if he was testing the waters she was open to his attentions. She held still in anticipation for several moments before feeling his leg press closer, followed by a tentative rubbing against her calf. She rubbed back, more than ready to make time with the young hunk.

His hairy leg moved between hers, and he slid closer, spooning his front to her back. For a brief moment she felt panicked, wondering when she'd last shaved her legs. What the hell that was about, she had no idea. The feeling was gone almost as soon as she acknowledged it, along with the realization it really didn't matter.

Once again the vision shifted and she was on her back, the guy lying draped over her, between her legs. He was tall, and had positioned himself so they were face to face, his abdomen pressing on her mons. They began to kiss and it was the strangest kiss she had ever experienced. He flattened out his tongue and kept up a rapid thrusting back and forth against hers. This particular caress would feel fabulous against her pussy lips, but was not doing anything for her mouth. Still, she wanted things to progress between them.

She considered herself to be well put together, and was happy with her appearance. How society thought women should look didn't matter to her. However, when faced with becoming intimate, Tamara felt nervous about how her partner would react to her rail-thin body, ribs and hip bones sticking out sharp and protruding against her skin. Her tiny breasts were no longer quite so perky due to time and gravity. She hated the insecurity which arose in these situations.

For some reason she wasn't worried in the least this time, which was amazing. It didn't matter that he was someone she'd tried with desperation to attract at one time. She accepted her body the way it was, flaws and all, without much concern for how he would react to those implied imperfections.

He pulled back after a while with a disappointed look on his handsome face. "You're not into this, are you?"

At this point she found herself wondering why the hell she'd lusted over him all those years ago because he was not very savvy when it came to seduction. Kissing was a skill you developed over time. Although he may not appreciate the criticism of his technique, she was going to have to teach him the art of the sensual kiss. After repositioning them with her on top, she aligned their bodies so her cunt rubbed against his erection then Tamara began showing him how to seduce her with a sultry kiss.

Her awareness slowly shifted from the dream world, although she was not yet fully awake either. Images, lessons and insights permeated her senses, replaying through her mind. She tried to hold on to the dream, searching for the meaning, reasons and wisdom before they slipped from her grasp.

Something told her the dream was significant to the changes she felt blooming to life within herself. Her easy acceptance of her body, seeing herself as she really was, not worrying if a partner would be turned off when seeing her naked. Add her being bold enough to instruct him how to pleasure her, and it all combined to blow her away. Maybe she was ready to accept herself the way she was, without recriminations.

What a startling idea. She let it play through her mind, trying it on for size as she came fully awake.

Almost as astonishing as the dream was the realization she was not lying on her bed in the cabin. Tamara sat up with dizzying quickness, surveying the area. The indirect sunlight hurt her bleary eyes. She lay on a soft layer of sweet-smelling hay, covered with a thin blanket. All around her was solid rock. Next to her, a small camp fire was burning, staving off the slight chill in the early morning air.

Damn, must have been some bender she went on last night.

Information filtered through her weary brain at a slow rate. Okay, she was somewhere out in the wilds of the mountains, lying in what appeared to be a large stone cavern. Against one wall sat an ice chest and several plastic bins, which she assumed contained food. Set out on top of one bin were several pieces of clothing she recognized as hers.

Fighting back the panic threatening to clog her throat, Tamara stood on shaky legs, and moved to the wide edge of the sheltered sleeping place. Stepping down a small slope, she turned in a wide circle to get a better look around.

It took several moments for her to assimilate the information and realize she was in a vast canyon surrounded by towering rock formations. The place where she'd been sleeping looked like a large crevice or indentation in the end of the canyon wall. Only two sides of the area were open, the rest was solid rock.

Shielding her eyes from the sun with her hand, she scanned the area. Dakota was nowhere in sight, yet she had vague memories of riding on a horse with him.

Holy shit! The crazy ass Indian went and left me alone in the middle of the wilderness.

Visions of all the animals she'd encounter in such a location assaulted her mind. The panic rose, tightening her chest and bringing the acidic taste of warm bile into her throat.

"Oh. My. God," she cried in a shrill tone. The high-pitched, trembling voice didn't sound like hers. The reverberations bounced across the canyon walls time and time again, bringing home how alone she was.

Struggling to remain calm, Tamara's mind ran through a million different possibilities in a matter of microseconds. There was no way she was about to set off into the wilds by herself not even knowing what direction to take. She'd heard stories of people wandering around lost in the mountains for weeks before dying of dehydration and starvation. Not an option.

Okay, girl. Think!

Expecting coherent thought was really asking for a lot. She had a horrible headache, and the need to empty her bladder was turning into an ache, making it difficult to think of anything else. What the hell was she supposed to do, pee in some bushes? She didn't delude herself into thinking there might be a bathroom somewhere near by. Damn, what she wouldn't give for some indoor plumbing right about now.

Looking around, Tamara spotted her boots near her makeshift bed. Something the cowboys had said about sleeping out in the wilderness filtered through her head. They had talked about finding snakes, scorpions, spiders, and other small, creepy creatures in their boots. Something about reptiles seeking out the warmth and shelter, and having to shake out their boots every morning.

The thought of turning over her boot and something slithering out made her shiver. Gross. She would not put her foot in there if some creature had been sleeping in her boot. Yet, she had no choice. She wasn't going to walk out into the wilderness wearing only her socks.

Damn it. She was going to kill Dakota when she found him. Rip the bastard limb from limb then chop up the pieces so small he'd never be found. The rotten bastard would pay for dumping her like this.

Maybe he had gone off somewhere to pee. Maybe he was even now bringing his horse and preparing to take her back to the ranch. Maybe...

CR&O

It took her forever to find a spot where she felt safe enough to drop her pants, exposing herself to all the beady little animal eyes she felt staring at her, and relieve her aching bladder.

Remembering other things she'd heard the cowboys say had her shaking the bushes and making as much noise as possible. It would be just her luck to drop her drawers and squat down only to have a snake strike out and bite her ass.

The very thought made her swing her head around in a frantic search for anything slithering in her direction. She could clearly picture the newspaper headlines. "City Girl Dies In Mountains From Venomous Bite On Bared Ass."

Yeah, getting bit would make her day from hell truly complete.

Tamara remained in a state of shock for quite a while. It was difficult for her to accept he'd left her alone with all her greatest fears. The whole thing seemed surreal, leaving her feeling out of touch. This was so far from anything she knew how to deal with. And there were no distractions to keep her from thinking too much.

Her mind worked overtime. After several hours of sitting on the bed of hay thinking, afraid to move, incredible pangs of unchecked emotion assaulted her. She wasn't used to dealing with her feelings. During most of this time she wept with uncontrollable anguish and unbearable pain. Huge sobs were wrenched from the very depths of her soul. Drawn out of her like an infection fought off by her body's natural immune system.

She didn't know what the tears and oppressive anguish were for, but they needed to be discarded. No matter how much she feared and detested the loss of control, there was nothing she could do to stop what had been set in motion. She was too far gone, her normal defenses nowhere to be found. Her only option was to ride out the ordeal.

There were still no signs of Dakota. Panic really sank its wicked claws into her, tearing away her fragile grip on what was real. How the hell was she supposed to survive out here all by herself?

It would be deathly quiet for long periods then small, furtive noises would begin all of a sudden. It freaked her out, making her pulse race and sending creepy-crawly sensations skittering over her skin. Yet the creatures stalking her never got brave enough to show themselves. For this small favor, she felt very grateful.

Her throat felt tight, her chest heavy, and an empty sensation plagued her stomach. She was tired, fatigued, bowels tied in knots, and her head pounded in a ceaseless drumming. There was no way she'd be able to eat anything, but she forced herself to drink two bottles of water she'd discovered in one of the plastic bins.

At one of her lowest points, feeling small and helpless, Tamara stood in the middle of the canyon, threw back her head and screamed. She cursed Dakota, his ancestors, and the horse he rode in on. Then she broke down and cried again.

So many things went through her mind since there wasn't much else to occupy her thoughts. She remembered bits and pieces of riding on the horse with Dakota as he fingered her to orgasm. That in itself was hard for her to accept. She had not been able to get off with only manual stimulation for ages, always requiring much more. Yet last night all she'd needed was the stroke of one man's thick fingers to send her rocketing into the most intense orgasm she'd ever experienced.

Had it really only been last night, or was it longer? She'd lost track of time.

For a while she felt guilty for the mess she'd made of her life. She carried so many ghosts and demons around with her, allowed the past to control her very existence for so long. She'd pushed people away, never giving more than a small piece of herself to anything or anyone. Not even to her dear friend, Savannah, who had given her everything. Well, at least she'd tried. Tamara never was very good at accepting anything she didn't get for herself.

Van had been happy to bring Tamara into her life, opening her home, and freely gave her friendship and love. What had she given in return? Nothing. Her inability to open herself to her friend left Tamara feeling...hollow.

For several hours she fought to keep her anger at bay, but it was all there was to hold on to. The anger filled up the empty place and allowed her to feel alive. Anything was better than feeling vacant.

All of this was Dakota's doing. *The bastard!* If it weren't for the damned Indian, she wouldn't be sitting here thinking about the past and trying to face all these jumbled emotions. Yes, it was all his fault. Tamara was steadfast in her refusal to accept responsibility for any of this mess. When she got a hold of the infuriating man...watch out. Shit would hit the fan and spread out to cover everyone and everything in her way.

It dawned on her then—she hadn't really lived or felt anything except sexual responses since childhood. Hell, for her to even feel something during sex required she make things increasingly wild, always taking things a step further in order to keep feeling something—anything. She went through the motions of life, but never partook in its true bounty.

Sheesh! She was starting to sound like one of those psychobabble self-help guides.

Over the rest of the long day and night, Tamara continued to mull over the dream visions and how her life was changing. It seemed as if the visions had been the final crack in an internal dam, setting free a flood of unwanted emotions.

She was blown away by the culmination of everything that had gradually happened. *What an incredible mind trip.*

Looking over the events of her life, she found a bit of understanding within her heart. She also discovered an acceptance of who and what she was. Hell, she was amazed to realize she was feeling comfortable in her own skin. This was something she'd never experienced before. And for once, Tamara felt free to live. So many things were changing, opening up, allowing her to breathe.

Whenever she got back to the ranch, things were going to change. She decided it was time to let Savannah know how much their friendship meant to her. And the cowboys—they had become an important force in her life. She harbored a deep, abiding love and caring for each one of her friends. Somehow she would find a way to express the emotions waiting for an outlet.

And Dakota. She had big plans for him.

A niggling doubt plagued her for a short time as to whether her friends would accept these alterations in her. She'd lived a certain way for so long. Some would try to keep her in the familiar niche she'd created where they knew what to expect from her.

By late on the second evening she'd dealt with her ghosts and faced down her demons, finding an odd feeling of contentment with a past she could not change and would no longer allow herself to remain feeling guilty over. There was no way she would alter her past even if it were possible. The past was quite simply the vehicle that had delivered her to this life-affirming point, created her, brought her to love.

In her moments of weakness, Tamara found an inner strength she'd never known existed within her. This was the most freeing experience she'd ever been through. More than anything, she wished Dakota was there to share it.

Just look at her, sitting in the middle of the wilds unafraid. It was miraculous. And she was able to be alone for the first time. Quiet contemplation was no longer a frightening prospect.

An overwhelming excitement filled her very being and replaced the void. She was anxious to embark on this new path. The only regret she had was for the wasted time, but it was an essential curve in the road.

Holy Shit! Was any of this real?

Oh, Dakota. I need you here with me. I want to share this with you so much.

At some point she slept, then awoke to witness the most dazzling sunrise. She wandered out into the canyon unafraid. Sitting next to the small stream, Tamara took in all the sounds of nature she'd never before appreciated.

The babbling sounds of water splashing over and against rock were unable to compete with the sharp, wild cries of winged creatures greeting the day. There was a unique hum and rhythm to the world she had never paid attention to before. Everything communicated in an almost silent harmony one had only to open their heart to hear.

The total and complete sense of oneness, peace and belonging filled her soul, lifting Tamara up on a gentle breeze. She felt as though she free-floated among the dazzling hues of gold, amber, garnet and plum painting the morning sky. Within her body, she felt the very hum and movement of earth and sky, spirit and life.

Chapter Seven

Morning found Dakota squatting still as a statue knee-deep in the cold stream. The frigid water was enough to make him grit his teeth. Add to this the screams of frustration carried on the crisp breeze over the last few days, and Dakota felt the desire to rip his own hair from his scalp. He was living the hell of her journey right along with Tamara, suffering through each emotion, and his nerves were shot.

No matter how much he'd wanted to go to his princess, wrap her up in his embrace to provide reassurance and shelter, he knew those comforts wouldn't help her. Tamara had to do this on her own. Facing down both her fears and the woman she'd become was a task she had to undertake alone.

Each cry and scream tore at his spirit. He would have been glad to take this on for her, take the pain into himself, if only he could. The fear, desperation and tired acceptance in her voice pierced his warrior's veneer, digging deep into his flesh.

Although he stayed far enough away to allow her this experience, Dakota was close by to ensure her safety. There was no doubt in his mind Tamara would wage a fierce war against any foe, but he would never forgive himself if something happened to her while she was stripped bare and vulnerable, fighting her inner battles.

Forcing himself to focus on the task at hand, he watched a wary trout hover in the crystal clear, life-sustaining waters. Each controlled, nimble movement revealed the power and strength of the determined fish, but as set as it was in its path, Dakota was equal in his determination to make the trout their dinner.

He waited with calm patience for the cautious fish to be right where he wanted it, summoning an inner fortitude, waiting for the perfect moment. The task required the same patience he must maintain for the sake of his mate. He began easing his hand closer behind the trout, letting it grow accustomed to this foreign presence. When the moment arrived, his hand was a mere blur of motion as it shot through the water, taking hold of the trout and hanging on as it struggled in vain to obtain its freedom once more.

He had spent time working with Hunter, exercising the horse's injured leg while standing in the shadows, keeping guard over her slight form. The boundless love he felt for this woman created an invisible connection, linking their spirits together. He felt every up and down she felt, and would know the moment she reached the completion of her passage.

Even then, instead of running straight into her arms, Dakota had enough wisdom to know she'd still need time to come to grips with the new emotions. Sexual needs rode him hard, making demands Tamara would not be ready to handle. For both their good he maintained his distance, giving her one last night, until the right moment arrived. His patience had worn thin with the rising of the sun. Now there would be nothing to stop him from claiming his spirit mate.

CR8O

The strength of his spirit filled her long before her eyes found him. Tamara gasped and rose to her feet in one swift movement. She watched his progress in quiet reverence for it was no mere man approaching. No, this was a proud warrior ripped from the past, transplanted into this time for her.

Lord, help her.

Dakota looked fierce and determined as he moved forward, pace steady and unhurried. He wore nothing save what appeared to be a bit of cloth covering his groin and his comfortable moccasins. The rest of his awe-inspiring body remained blessedly bare. From one large hand dangled a string of fish.

His expression was hidden from her by the bright sunlight illuminating his body from behind. Dark hair hung unbound, bouncing about his shoulders with each movement. She saw some type of strap running at an angle across his broad chest from one shoulder to the opposite side of his abdomen.

The tattoo on his arm stood out, illuminated by the bright morning light. She almost expected to see the feathers on his biceps flutter, stirred by the gentle breeze. He appeared much as she would imagine Native American warriors of another time had looked when returning home after the hunt. It was a sight she would not soon forget. Her very own hero returned with his kill.

Amazing and frightening in the same instant!

Her heart pounded, performing flip-flops within her chest. The ache of inner longing set her blood aflame. One touch and she would dissolve into a puddle at his feet, worshiping before the magnificent man.

A rush of foreign emotions filled Tamara, holding her spellbound, and she knew they emanated straight from Dakota. She felt a deep sense of wonder and pride, compassion and understanding, patience and longing. Somehow the cacophonous feelings came together in overall relief and harmony. What she felt toward him was immense yet uncomplicated. Love, pure and simple.

Never in her life had she harbored such intense impressions of belonging and unconditional love. She knew deep in her heart no matter what, Dakota would always be there offering quiet acceptance.

An intoxicating surge of elation buoyed her vitality as he stalked toward her, moving with an animalistic grace. Although she wanted to hurtle herself into his arms, she was frozen to the spot, a helpless observer.

As he drew near, broad shoulders blocking out the sun, she took in the blissful, radiant smile softening his strong features. Dakota appeared as ecstatic as she felt.

Tamara attempted to speak, but her voice came out broken, and she struggled to control her quivering arms and legs. She was determined not to dissolve into a useless blob of emotional female. Reaching deep within herself, she found a reservoir of strength and determination, and drew upon it.

She cleared her throat and began again. "There is so much I want to tell you, so much I have to share that I don't know where to begin. And yet, I think you already know. I have the feeling if anyone can understand what is happening to me, it's you."

Dakota didn't speak as he stared into her eyes. Reaching out, he took her hand and placed it over his heart, holding it captured beneath his own hand. He remained silent for a moment as she absorbed the rhythm of his life force.

"Close your eyes and use your other senses," he said, speaking in a soft, reverent tone. "Feel the swish created by my heart with each contraction and expansion it makes. See the connection between our hearts in your mind's eye. Feel the echo of each beat move through your hand, up your arm, into your own body. Notice the crazed beating of your own heart slowing to match mine."

He was right, she did feel it. Almost as if they were becoming one. It was a transforming sensation, almost overwhelming. Yet having the physical connection with him grounded her, providing vibes of well-being.

"Take a deep breath and smell the air. In that breath you will detect not only both of our individual scents, but the scent of the very earth with which we are one."

She took a shuddering breath, a sudden rush of adrenaline coursing through her veins as she appreciated how the two of them were connected to everything around them. She smelled all of those things combined together to make one whole, binding them with an invisible thread.

Dakota's firm lips brushed against her own.

"Open. Taste me. Let the flavor roll over your tongue and fill you."

With blind obedience she opened her mouth to receive his kiss, drinking him in, consumed by a greedy thirst for which she would not apologize. It was the same exotic, somewhat spicy taste she recognized, yet it was different—probably because *she* was different.

Their tongues stroked each other's before swirling together, taking in everything the other gave and giving back more. When Dakota's tongue withdrew from her mouth, she followed it into his, beginning her own thorough explorations, realizing he tasted like home. When he broke away, she whimpered at the loss.

"Now, open your eyes. Your spirit and your heart recognize me as your spirit mate. Let your eyes roam over my face and body. Let the recognition seep deep into your very cells."

Following his instructions, she let her gaze move over his familiar countenance. What she had run from was unmistakable. It had been there all along—this soul-deep connection both frightened and fortified her. It went beyond rational thought, requiring a leap of faith, trust. In that moment Tamara realized she did believe in Dakota.

What a strange, foreign feeling. It was a brand new occurrence. Finding sexual release was no longer so important to her now. Not if it came without the emotional connection she understood would come from making love with him. What was it he had called them, spirit mates? The words sounded right.

"Your spirit is the sixth sense. It recognizes and perceives information about your existence that doesn't come through the five tangible senses. Your spirit responds, reacts, and filters what you experience by using your other senses. This is also what makes you who you are."

Okay, she got it. She saw how all these things were interconnected with the whole—how the two of them were connected together. What a wonderful concept. Tamara had not felt a true link to anyone or anything in the past. Yet here and now, she shared an indelible union with this magnificent man. Her heart felt ready to burst with the abundance of new feelings bombarding it.

"Now that you've allowed your spirit and heart to heal, you can begin to live and love once again in peaceful harmony between body, land, sky and spirit."

A bit of fear still lingered. Did she dare allow herself to hope the love and tangible bond she shared with this man was a good thing, something she'd be able to count on? Dare she hope to give up all her hang-ups? The strength of the unfamiliar outlook bewildered as much as it gave hope and inspired her. Every instinct she possessed was leaning in the same direction. Dakota was the one man alive who would love and accept her, help her to be everything she was meant to be.

Could she accept such a foreign idea?

She had a powerful, overwhelming need to be with him in every way possible a woman could be with a man. Not in the ways she had fucked others. This need was different. She needed more than the physical release his body would bring to hers. Tamara wanted all the emotional trappings which went along with making love. The one problem—she had no idea where to even begin. She had never made love with anyone before. The entire concept was alien to her. The ache created by her needs went much further than her physical body, and she had no idea what to do about them.

"Dakota," she whimpered. Her voice conveyed a small measure of the desperation she felt.

"Shh. I know, princess. I will help you. It'll be all right now," he soothed.

Taking her hand and raising it to his lips, he pressed a gentle kiss against her fingers before leading her toward the shelter. Once there, he made a quick survey of the supplies, making note of how little she had used.

"First thing we need to do is feed you."

Tamara's entire body trembled with the needs she was unable to contain. "But, Dakota..."

Returning to her side, Dakota guided her to the pallet and sat her down. "You have used up your energy reserves, princess. When we come together, you're going to require all the strength you can get. So first you will eat, then we'll make love and join our spirits."

The husky, raw quality to his deep voice reached right into her body, spreading a wave of arousal from the roots of her hair all the way down to her toenails. "Hurry, please!"

Sitting on the primitive bed, she watched him move around the small space after removing the pouch from his back. Each action was performed with an economy of motion. She was mesmerized by the play of hard muscle under dark cinnamon skin. The desire to run her fingers over all that glorious, bare male flesh made her palms itch. She wanted to rip the scrap of loincloth from around his hips, freeing the rest of him to her hungry eyes.

Dakota was focused on preparing the food. In no time flat he had a fire going with the fish filleted and sizzling away. In another pan a mixture of fresh vegetables was simmering along with some exotic-smelling seasonings, which he had taken from the pouch. One of the ice chests became a table when covered with a piece of cloth. Before she had time to contemplate the preparation of such a meal, Dakota had a veritable feast spread out before them.

As soon as she began nibbling at the delights overflowing the large plate, Tamara realized she was ravenous. Everything tasted so fresh and flavorful. In part it was due to having foods fresh from the earth instead of coming from cellophane-wrapped packages in the grocery store. Part of the flavor also came from Dakota's cooking skills. She figured a good portion also came from her new appreciation for the simplest of things.

The feel of sunlight caressing her skin now created a warm glow spreading throughout her entire being. She found a great enjoyment in watching the small animals that used to frighten her as they scurried around. A whole new world was opening up before her, and Tamara didn't want to miss a single thing.

They discussed these new revelations as they ate and for the first time in her life, she didn't feel the need to fill pauses in conversation with frivolous chatter. There was no longer a fear of pondering things over in her mind because the past no longer ruled her.

She felt liberated and unburdened, free and right with the universe. Incredible!

After eating their meal, they washed the pans, dishes and utensils in the stream. They even shared some playful antics in the water, laughing with one another. Whatever came natural was what they allowed to happen, but still the longing and sexual need grew within her until she couldn't stand it anymore. She knew this man wanted scary things like love, commitment, and forever from her. She would gladly give all that and more just to have him make love with her.

Looking up at him from under thick, lush lashes, she whispered, "Dakota, I need you...now." Her look of desperation punctuated the plea, letting him know the extremity of her craving for him.

Chapter Eight

The time was right. Dakota felt almost nervous and shy. Yet the anticipation of making love with his spirit mate, making their bond permanent, chased away all other thoughts. He meant to cherish every second. Before he was done, he'd know every inch of her body and all its sweet contradictions. From her thin arms with their firm biceps all the way down to her dainty yet sturdy feet. He would leave no part of her undiscovered.

The heated look in her beautiful green eyes, their dark pupils enlarged with desire, sent blood rushing straight to his cock. He wanted to rip off her clothes and sink into the warmth of her body, but somehow he would find the restraint to lavish her with his love. By the time he was finished, Tamara would have no doubt he'd made love with her and they would always be together. Even if maintaining restraint killed him.

He wanted to lay her down right where they stood. Instead, he drew on his inner calm, walking her back to the pallet bed. Standing there, sheltered from the sun's harsh rays, he became lost in the emotions he read in her expressive eyes. There was no doubt in his mind she knew how special this first time would be, and was anticipating it as much as he did.

Using the pad of his thumb, Dakota caressed the curve of her pouty bottom lip, relishing the small tremor coursing through the soft flesh. Bending his head, he maintained eye contact, cupping her precious face in his hands and moving closer until their breath mingled.

Sharing the same air was a heady experience. Their breathing quickened. Neither of them wanted to wait for the next shared breath, the next touch driving their need even higher.

Framing her face in the warmth of his hands, he let his thumbs caress her prominent cheekbones. His entire body trembled. Dakota felt as though their spirits had brushed up against each other and the world stood still in silent observance of the magnitude of emotions generated by the brief but monumental touch. Knowing the moment lasted no longer than the space between one heartbeat and the next did not lessen its impact.

When he moved in and their lips met, time slowed and the world held its breath. Everything about the moment would forever be imprinted on his lips, his flesh and blood—the spirit driving him. Her soft sigh of appreciation made his blood sing. His attention was held rapt by the tiny catch in her throat as her breathing stopped. When it picked back up she was breathing twice as fast, and he reveled in the racing of Tamara's pulse beneath the fingers trailing down her slender neck.

At first he simply pressed his lips to hers, enjoying their warmth and texture, his entire focus narrowed down to the sweet, delicate point of contact. With gentle pressure, he sucked her bottom lip between his. Great Spirit...it felt so right. His knees shook as first chills and then a wave of heat surged through his body. A tremor of equal parts ache and ecstasy began in his abdomen, quickly spreading outward. It was so unbearable and sweet Dakota had tears forming at the corners of his eyes.

The sound of a wise spirit's voice trailed through his head.

You will cling to this moment in time for the rest of your days. Joining with your spirit mate will forever more be the memory you draw strength from. Let it seep into you, becoming part of the very fabric of your being.

That was exactly what he did. Every nuance of the way she responded to him was so natural, giving everything she was. These moments would sustain him in the leanest of times. The sweet, distinctive taste of her lips would forever be his greatest craving.

When the tip of his tongue caressed the succulent treat he'd captured, her soft sigh let him know how profound an effect the light contact had on her. A tender nibbling had her opening for him. Even when her lips parted in an attempt to deepen their connection, Dakota maintained the tender caress until he was no longer able to resist temptation, immersing himself in their kiss. With the thoroughness he reserved for the most important tasks, he began a deliberate seduction of the warm haven he found.

Every fine hair on his body stood on end as he took her into himself with methodical care. First he learned the texture and taste of the sensitive flesh between her lips and teeth. With a gradual progression, he explored each tooth where slick, smooth areas contrasted the ridges and peaks. Every sensation, taste and texture was burned indelibly into his memory as his tongue slid along each delicious new discovery.

Tamara met every caress of lips and tongue, pouring herself into the mating of their mouths. The rapid rise and fall of her breasts as she pressed in close against his chest made him ache with a need like nothing else he'd known, stirring desires difficult to control. He mustered every ounce of restraint to maintain the tortuous slow pace, but what a sweet torment it was. She put so much of herself into the soul-deep kiss, she had to lean her weakened body into his for support.

Letting his hands glide down her arms until reaching her waist, Dakota lifted her, easing the crick in his neck from holding the stooped-over position for so long. For someone with such an abundant spirit, her body was so small and fragile within his grasp, reminding him to take care. As he eased his grip, the siren brushed her hardened nipples over his chest, causing him to reflexively tighten his hold once again. His fingers flexed against her hips, a drawn-out purr reverberating through his chest and into her mouth.

They engaged in an age-old dance of advance and retreat, each following where the other led while devouring every nuance of the rapturous joining. Their passion became more fevered with each caress, bodies plastered as close as possible. When he lay her down on the pallet, both of them took great gasping breaths before sinking into each other once again.

He'd never known such incredible bliss like he experienced when her small hands began to learn his body, touching everywhere within reach, giving even more than she took. With each delicate, potent caress against his inflamed skin their shared passion rose to new, dazzling heights. Angling their hips, he pressed his painful erection against the blazing heat between her thighs. Tamara wrapped her legs around him, holding on with improbable strength.

She whimpered as he lifted his torso, grabbing hold of her thin top. Dakota drew out the task and let his gaze devour each inch of creamy flesh revealed as he slid the garment up her body. He delighted in the way the hoop through her navel jiggled with the trembling of her abdomen. The material rasped over swollen nipples, and he thrilled with the resulting hissed intake of breath between the tight clench of teeth. The sensual sound sent shivers racing through him.

He flung the shirt, oblivious as to where it landed, not willing to remove his eyes from the veritable feast of her exquisite body. How the hell would he ever survive until he managed to immerse himself in his mate?

The thin grip he held on his control was slipping as he struggled to hold himself in check. He wanted to take this slow, to worship every delectable treat laid out before him, but her incessant writhing beneath him might waylay those desires. Each small movement created the most wonderful friction between her warm mound and his aching cock.

The connection between them sizzled and crackled in the crisp air. Staring into her glassy eyes, Dakota lowered his mouth to her lips once again for a light butterfly kiss, then paid rapt attention to the minutest details as he teased the swirls of her ear. His restraint was pushed to its limits, his delicate licks and kisses becoming interspersed with nibbles and bites.

Each lustful noise his efforts elicited from his princess created a celebration within his spirit, sending it soaring to the heavens and back again. Her responsiveness was everything he'd ever dreamed of and so much more. The link between them grew stronger as her fingers tightened in his hair, the slight pain grounding him as her soft body arched against his hard one.

Dakota's lips made a slow trek down the graceful length of neck to tease her shoulder. The notch at the base of her throat tempted him, meriting extra attention to be lavished upon it. As he made his way along her prominent collarbone, he almost felt the sensations his loving evoked within her.

He teased her without mercy, spending long moments consuming the smooth curves of her breasts, ignoring the places she tried to draw his attentions. When at last he arrived at her left nipple, Tamara's cry of need pierced his heart.

Hesitating only a moment longer, he gloried in her shivers as his warm breath caressed the turgid peak.

"Please," she whispered.

"Tell me, princess. What do you want? What do you need? Turn it all over to me."

Her fingers slid through his hair, fisting in the silky strands as she struggled with the frenzy of want and tangled desires. As the warmth of his tongue stroked over her nipple, she arched her back and pulled his head closer. It thrilled him to see the goose bumps break out over her skin as his amused chuckle rippled through his body to be absorbed by hers.

"Everything! I want it all. Please, don't make me wait any longer."

Before the words had died away, he sucked the delicious peak into the warmth of his mouth. Tamara flexed her hips, rubbing her clit against the hard length of his cock. She ground against him as he moved from one rich coral nipple to the other, stroking and kneading her small tits with his hands.

Each movement became more frantic as she rocketed out of control on an express train, ready to crest the highest of mountains. He enjoyed the ecstasy glowing on her beautiful face as she plunged headlong into a stunning orgasm.

As corny as it sounded, even hearing it in her own head, Tamara was certain she'd felt the earth move beneath her. Dakota seemed to be the one man able to bring her to orgasm with little effort, yet no matter how small the exertion, she was overwhelmed by the sensations and emotions he elicited with such skill.

It had been hell trying to contain her shuddering breaths, struggling to hold back the whimpering noises coming from somewhere deep inside her, expressing pleas she was not yet comfortable voicing. Although, in an unfamiliar way it felt safe to let her supplication be revealed to him.

Tamara was not accustomed to verbally expressing desires and needs. She was much more comfortable with physically directing and controlling sexual play, thus keeping her weaknesses hidden. Being a dominant player was a normal role for her in bed. This was vastly different, a new experience, the quiet pleas seeming to leave her exposed, relinquishing her needs to his loving care. She felt disconcerted by how easy it was becoming to turn everything over to him.

She trusted Dakota was not a man who would use her obvious surrender against her, other than as a guide in bestowing even greater pleasure. Where this inherent conviction came from, she had no idea. It went against all her life lessons to believe in or rely upon another, yet she found herself giving him her implicit trust.

A million diverse, contradictory feelings were battling for supremacy within her. She was frightened of this uncharted emotional territory. Having never given all of herself to anyone before, there was no map for her to follow, no signs to give her direction. The "L" word kept popping into her mind, trying to escape past her lips. The thought of admitting to such an emotion and actually speaking the words out loud was beyond frightening, bordering on being an alien domain.

There were snippets of memories from her childhood which brought back a sense of having been loved and cared for, but they were too distant and fleeting to help her now in this situation.

But she was not alone, and felt safe giving herself over to his care. Dakota surrounded her with warmth, tenderness and scorching passion. While she was not accustomed to listening to her heart, it reassured her he wouldn't allow her to fall or be hurt. Instead, he'd protect and cherish her with everything he had.

In the past, sex had always been for sport—a recreational activity to help blow off steam. There were never any real attachment. But now everything was changing. This was so deviant from her norm—it went without saying what they shared was not just a mindless roll in the hay. They were creating an indelible emotional bond.

Some scary shit, for sure!

His deep, soothing voice broke into her mental musings. "Are you okay, princess?"

The depth of affection and concern in his dark eyes almost stopped her heart. Tamara wasn't certain how she'd ever survive this. Then her personal motto flashed through her mind.

When all else fails, give 'em attitude!

"Mmm...just getting warmed up, stud. That was a nice appetizer. I'm ready for the entrée now."

His throaty laughter almost succeeded in breaking down her hasty attempt at self-preservation. Damn, this man posed a great threat to her natural defenses.

"Okay, baby. Let's see if I can do something to fill you up and satisfy those hunger pangs."

The double entendre had her blood heating and moisture pooling between her thighs. Yes, she'd like to be filled. The sooner the better. It was time to kick this delightful ride into full gear.

"Well, ride 'em, cowboy," she taunted in a superior tone of voice.

His penetrating gaze seemed to take her measure as he decided how to respond. She wanted to groan out loud with frustration when he did speak again in careful, measured tones.

"Not so fast, princess. We're going to take this nice and slow, spend some time really getting to know each other."

Aw, hell. He meant to continue torturing her with a slow seduction. But she still had some tricks up her sleeve. One way or another she'd quicken his pace. With the thought held firm in mind, she went forward, eyes wide open.

The solid weight of his body still covering hers ignited new desires. It didn't matter she'd found release moments ago, she needed more to be satisfied. A whole lot more. Tamara was determined to get exactly what she wanted.

Cupping the sides of her breasts in his warm hands, Dakota lowered his head into the meager valley of her cleavage. He turned from side to side with tender movements, caressing the soft flesh with his cheeks. His thumbs stroked a delicate pattern over her nipples and she arched her back, bringing about a firmer contact. The simple petting touch was beyond extraordinary.

Of their own volition, her fingers wound themselves into his silky hair once again, holding him in place. For some reason the casual, tender way he touched her fired her desires, evoking unfamiliar needs as she lost herself in the rapture of his lovemaking.

Before the realization took root in her mind that this was the crux of the juxtaposition, making love as opposed to having sex, she was swept away. Coherent contemplation had become impossible as all thoughts melted away and her body took control.

She had to feel him held deep inside her, locked tight within her body.

"Dakota!"

"Hush, I've got you, Tamara."

His attention remained focused on her swollen breasts and engorged nipples. Each tender touch and loving kiss created rivers of blazing heat sliding down her abdomen, pooling between her legs. Tiny nerve endings sprang back to life, her pussy lips and clit swelling. The heat rolling off his body only intensified the fire growing within her.

Shifting lower, at last heading the direction she wanted him to go, Dakota began tracing lazy yet intricate patterns over the quivering flesh of her abdomen. Closing her eyes, she tried to concentrate and envision the figures he drew with his tongue, but it wasn't working. All she thought about was having his tongue licking her clit and plunging into her cunt.

She wanted him to take everything, draw her deep inside his body and merge together into one. Then she wanted to start from the beginning again and again, over and over until neither one of them had enough strength left to even lift a finger.

Chapter Nine

Everything he had, everything he was, went into cherishing Tamara's beautiful body. An exponential increase in her allure occurred when the bright light of her spirit began shining through the exterior trappings, captivating Dakota.

Using the tip of his tongue and fingers, he traced the shapes of constellations on her skin. As a child, he'd learned about life and his people—where they came from, were going, even how they'd lived—through stories written in the stars. He imagined when he looked up upon those dazzling, guiding lights tonight he'd see something different written there for both of them. It was not possible to go through such a profound life-altering experience as joining with your spirit mate without forever being changed.

Struggling to ignore the incessant ache in his cock, which demanded that he complete their joining, Dakota took his time investigating his mate. Her scent was an intoxicating combination of the world around them and her own unique, feminine scent. To him, she smelled like home. From her shiny, mahogany strands of hair all the way to her dainty, painted toenails, she was his life, his heart, his future.

Her fair skin was softer than velvet beneath his fingers, and tasted like the sweet nectar of a ripe peach on his tongue. In his mind's eye, he envisioned their child taking sustenance from her breast, hungry mouth latched onto the round, coral areola. As his tongue teased the silver loop at her navel, he imagined countless hours lying with his head on the slope of her belly, rounded and full with their babe.

Catching the waistband of her cotton shorts with his fingers, he slid the material over slim hips, down the length of her legs and past her feet. Her tiny whimpers tested what strength he had left, but Dakota would not be denied. Cradling her foot in his hands, he began to work his way back up her petite body at a casual pace.

Tamara moaned as he kissed the arch of her foot, then gasped when he sucked a tiny toe into his mouth. She writhed with restless need on the pallet as he teased the tender flesh of her instep and ankle. Murmuring ancient words of comfort against her skin, he tasted every luscious inch, pausing whenever he found a sensitive spot to lavish with his attentions. He left no treasure undiscovered as he learned his mate's body and her responses.

The soft hollow behind her knee drove him to distraction, but the tender flesh of her inner thighs beckoned. Each movement over her gorgeous body brought him closer to the heat of her core where the musky scent of her arousal drove him wild. He didn't know how much longer he'd manage to hold back.

"Dakota, please!" Tamara shrieked as he nipped at her thigh.

"Relax, princess. I'll get there."

Looking over the length of her torso, he noticed she was no longer waiting for him, but had taken matters into her own hands in a literal way. Her small hands massaged her breasts, fingers plucking at her nipples. The mere sight of her back arching, driving her breasts into her palms, was close to being his undoing.

Great Spirit! He wanted nothing more than to rip off his loincloth and sink into the heat of her body. With her knees bent as they were, he was able to see the moisture covering her bare pussy and inner thighs. The pink folds were open and inviting, her engorged clit peeking out from under its hood.

Drawing on his inner spiritual strength, he took a deep breath and continued on his path. They would have the rest of their lives for wild abandon, but only this one first time. He didn't want it to be some fast, hurried fuck.

The first taste of her sweet cream on his tongue nearly killed him. As he laved the arousal from the crease of her thigh, Tamara's fingers fisted painfully in his hair. With firm tugs, she attempted to guide his mouth where she wanted it most.

He lifted her legs onto his shoulders, wrapping his biceps under her thighs and folding his forearms over her hips to still her bucking movements. His arms were long enough his fingers came together along the sides of her slit. Spreading her open, he took his time tasting every fold, discovering each tender morsel of flesh. Her mindless pleading made him smile, as did her efforts to move her hips, struggling against his tight hold.

No longer able to stand the delay himself, he thrust his tongue into her moist depths and made teasing circles around her clit with his finger while drinking in the heady juices of her response. His cock felt like a hard stick of dynamite ready to explode. Attempts to soothe the throbbing flesh by rubbing against the edge of the pallet only made him harder. Taking this slow just might kill him.

Tamara was going to lose it if the devil between her legs didn't touch her clit soon. There were no two ways about it. The tiny bundle of nerves stood at attention, aching for his touch, but Dakota's finger only circled around her needy flesh.

Convulsions shot through her muscles, milking his tongue. She needed more. The thought of him driving his cock into her cunt had her squirming against the tight hold of his arms. Each movement sent the cool, satin strands of his long hair tickling over her heated skin like the soft caress of butterfly wings.

As his tongue plundered her depths, she felt his nose nudge her clit and she neared an explosive state. If he pressed a little firmer she'd reach completion. She'd tugged on his hair endlessly, but it did no good. He seemed to be intent upon keeping her hanging by the edge of her fingernails, torturing her without relief.

Another gentle nudge with his nose had her gasping and cussing. "Damn you. Touch my clit," she ordered.

"Not yet, princess."

His light chuckle of laughter, coupled with the nickname, pissed her off. She growled and writhed, fighting with desperation for the one touch that would unleash the pent-up volcano ready to blow.

"Dakota...you bastard. Fuck me!"

Nothing worked to get a response out of the crazy Cowboy-Indian driving her insane. Cursing, pleading, struggling—it was no use. He continued his relaxed tasting at her expense.

The instant he loosened his grip to change position, Tamara sprung into action but Dakota had anticipated her move. He unhooked his arms from her legs, pinning her beneath his forearms and upper body. This gave him more freedom to move his hands. Thick fingers spread her swollen lips again, and for a moment nothing happened. The devil stared at her open pussy, his breath caressing her flesh in a cool wave. A spasm shot through her clit at the stimulus, yet left her perched on the edge.

Her world dissolved as Dakota flashed a sinful grin then leaned forward. He captured the neglected bundle of nerves between his lips, sucking the flesh into his mouth with firm pulls. She felt the sting of his teeth as he latched onto her clit, followed by the electric stroke of his tongue.

Her eyes snapped shut, millions of pinpoints of light bursting behind her clamped lids as she surged over the precipice at last. Tamara heard herself scream the diabolical torturer's name as endless spasms shot through her flesh. Wave after wave of pleasure tore through her body, leaving her in a state of complete satiation as her orgasm subsided.

Damn, but was he good!

Exhaustion plagued her as she came back to her senses. Small aftershocks detonated through her quivering clit as the powerful rush faded. Tamara found the fiendish rogue staring at her, a wicked smile playing across his sensual lips. Her cream coated his mouth and chin.

He looked so fucking sexy.

She watched with intent curiosity as he rose between her trembling thighs, finally shucking off the scrap of cloth covering his groin. The divine sight of Dakota naked would have driven her to her knees, had she not already been lying down.

Disheveled strands of dark hair framed his handsome face. It was a strong, caring face capable of expressing deep emotion, which Tamara knew she would never tire of seeing. She read insatiable lust in his desire-darkened eyes and the tight clench of his jaw.

Her eyes traveled down the thick column of his neck to broad shoulders capable of carrying the weight of the world with ease. She drank in every detail of the way he looked.

Muscular arms and torso, rigid abdomen, trim hips, and... Oh. My. God!

With his left hand, he stroked the most sumptuous cock with casual confidence. The satiny skin over the steely shaft was a shade darker than the rest of his skin, the head a deep, ruddy color. Thick blue veins engorged the flesh with blood. The base was thicker than the shaft, ending in an uncut foreskin below the large crown. Each stroke of his hand created a game of peek-a-boo with the head of his cock, revealing it on the back stroke, covering it again with each forward stroke. It was an incredible sight.

"Holy shit," she blurted in amazed wonder. "You've got a hoodie."

How delightful. She'd never seen an uncircumcised cock before, but found it to be a mouthwatering thing to behold. Tamara pictured taking his beautiful cock in her mouth and laving the sensitive area protected by the foreskin when flaccid.

Dakota groaned at the images created in his mind as the pink tip of her tongue slid across her lips. There was no way he would survive the sinful pleasures of her wicked mouth right now, though. Not without exploding and shooting his come down her throat. They would have to save such sweet pleasure for later. He wanted to be buried balls deep in her hot pussy.

"We'll try a taste test later," he stated with arrogance. "Right now, I need to be inside you and feel your pussy cling to my cock."

His princess offered no objection. Need filled her darkened green eyes as she bent her knees and spread her legs wide.

"Don't make me wait any longer." Desire had tightened her throat so the words were a mere whisper.

Kneeling between her thighs, Dakota used his own legs to push hers wider. His hands slid under her ass, massaging the firm muscles before lifting her hips high above the pallet.

When he lowered his weight over her, Tamara expected him to plunge his hard shaft straight into her. She was surprised when he leaned forward and took her mouth in the sweetest of kisses, sharing the depth of his affection. By the time he pulled back, they were both panting for breath.

"There is no going back, Tamara." His voice was husky with emotion, his expression serious. "Once we join together, I'll never let you go."

She had no doubt he'd honor the statement. The words were reflected in the turbulent black depths of his eyes where she witnessed his conviction. This man meant forever.

"If you can't accept that, tell me now."

Her heart lodged in her throat and a tremor spread through her body. Never in her life had she even allowed herself to dream of such a man, and such a proposition. It was beyond comprehension. Dakota was offering her the world on a silver platter. All she had to do was reach out and grab hold.

For the briefest of moments, Tamara worried she was not a forever kind of woman, but then she looked into his eyes again. What she saw melted the icy shell protecting her heart. In those fathomless black pools she caught a glimpse of the future. Dakota would give her complete and total devotion, unconditional acceptance, nonstop passion, and love without limits. Everything she'd never let herself hope to find, never knew she desired.

Opening her arms in welcome, she struggled to find the words to express the overwhelming tide of emotion surging to life within her splintered spirit. "Yes," she croaked, then cleared her voice. When she spoke again, her voice was stronger and held a deep sincerity. "I want it all. Everything you have, and everything I can give in return."

Before the words were even out of her mouth, she felt the broad head of his cock press against her spread opening. Slight movements of his hips had his cock stroking along her heated slit, coating himself in the abundance of her hot juices.

Gripping his biceps, Tamara implored him, "Please, Dakota. Now!"

He was certain it was difficult for her not to break from his impassioned gaze, but she wouldn't avert her gaze. When his hips thrust forward, her eyes widened and she gasped. The walls of her pussy gripped his cock, pulling him into her depths like they'd done with his tongue.

He held stock still for only a moment, giving them both a chance to adjust, savor their initial joining. When he thrust forward again, he seated his cock within his princess to the hilt. His spirit soared into the heavens, and a feeling of rightness settled over him. Pulling back, his cock slid from her pussy until only the head remained in her warm embrace, then he began a slow rhythm of advance and retreat, punctuating each forward drive with words of devotion.

"Everything...forever...my heart...my spirit...always."

Tamara gripped his sides with her thighs. Her heels dug into his ass as she clung tight to anchor her movements, meeting each thrust, holding nothing back. She took his mouth in a kiss she knew fell short of expressing what was in her heart. As their lips separated, she struggled to find the words. Words she'd never used and didn't know how to utter. Instead, she followed his example, repeating his oath back to him, adding in her own twist.

"Everything...forever...my heart...my spirit...always, my love."

What drove her to speak those last two words was beyond her grasp at the moment, but they felt right. Even if she couldn't say I love you, the sentiment would let him know she did.

Their thrusts became harder, Dakota sinking deeper into her very being each time he drove into her body. With each plunge, his pelvic bone ground down against her clit creating the most wonderful friction. Their combined need intensified as they rocketed toward a monumental implosion that would meld them together forever.

A fierce roar rumbled up from his chest. She had the fleeting impression he looked very much like a grizzly bear, but his words were quick to drive all thought from her mind.

"Come for me...with me," Dakota growled.

Lowering her hands from his arms to the clenching cheeks of his ass, Tamara held on tight. "Yes. Now, Dakota," she cried as the orgasm swept through her body. "Come in me...fill me," she gasped.

Her internal muscles clamped down on his cock, fighting to stop the shallow strokes and keep him deep within her body. The next thing she knew, she was flooded with the warmth of his come as he threw back his head and bellowed his release to the heavens.

He continued to rock his semi-hard shaft into her pussy until the last of the lingering aftershocks faded away. With gentle care, he lowered her back to the pallet, resting his weight over her body. Tamara reveled in the feeling of lying beneath his comforting mass. In the past, the first thing on her mind after sex was a shower. Right now the only thing she considered was the man covering her with his warmth. They were both sweaty and sticky, but she didn't care.

Dakota stirred, rising up on his elbows and looking down into her face. His fingers came up to brush damp, matted strands of dark hair away.

Tamara wanted to profess her feelings, but the words still stuck in her throat. She found it would take a hell of a lot of courage to utter those three little words, and contented herself with waiting a while longer to say them.

Chapter Ten

"There's no way in hell she would have set out of here on foot," Brock bellowed into the phone for the third time. Why the dense, jackass sheriff's deputy didn't understand was beyond him. "She wouldn't take off for three days alone without telling someone either. And Tamara is not comfortable with nature, especially not when facing it alone."

The moron had the nerve to guffaw at the statement, which only increased his exasperation. His obtuse comments were beginning to make Brock's blood boil.

"Why does she live smack dab in the middle of nature on a ranch then, huh?"

Jerk off. "Look, let me spell it out for you. Tamara Dobbs is a city girl. She lives out here 'cause this is where her friends live. Yes, once in a while she disappears for a few days at a time, but never for this long. And never on foot!" Brock raked his fingers through his mussed-up hair for about the hundredth time since initiating the conversation. "Something has happened to her."

Millie, Riley, Zeke and Jesse were all trying to interject their comments and opinions. Brock waved them off. It was understandable they were all riled up, but it wasn't helping the situation at all.

The deputy's voice became serious. "Now, wait a minute. Didn't you also tell me that your new employee, the Indian, is also gone? They probably just went off for some fun and games."

Okay, that did it. His patience had reached its limits. This insignificant, wet-behind-the-ears idiot had pushed him too far.

"Dakota has taken some medical R&R time. There is no way Tamara is with him. It doesn't fit. Something has happened to her. I want someone out here within the hour to file a missing persons report and start an investigation." The order came out in a gruff tone, leaving no room for argument.

"All right, settle down now. I'll talk to..."

"Listen to me," Brock growled. "Either you get someone competent out here now, or I'm coming down there."

For the space of several heartbeats no one said a word as the threat hung in the air. When he spoke again, the deputy seemed to have given up fighting him, taking on a more sober tone.

"Um...you're talking about the Shooting Star ranch, right?"

"That's right." Brock smacked his forehead in frustration. He heard a muffled conversation going on in the background for several moments before the deputy spoke again with an adjusted attitude. Hell, the man seemed downright contrite.

"Sheriff Monroe just returned to the office. He asked me to let you know he's personally heading out there right now. I apologize for any delay in our response. Please assure the Blacks this situation will be taken seriously and handled quickly."

A smug grin curved up the edges of his mouth. Sheriff Monroe was a personal friend of Van's. Since the very capable lawman was now involved, Brock knew the matter would be given the serious attention it deserved.

"That'll be fine. If he gets here quick enough, I may even forget to tell the sheriff what a total imbecile you are."

He hung up the phone with a loud thunk then turned to his impatient friends.

"Sheriff is on his way out. I think it's time to tell Cord and Van what's going on." After each of them nodded their agreement, he placed the phone call he'd dreaded making. There was no way he wanted to interrupt their honeymoon, but he knew Tamara was very important to Van and she'd want to know what was happening.

CRSD

Cord and Savannah didn't arrive back at the ranch until after the sheriff had already come and gone. Upon stepping out of the Hummer, they were surrounded by their worried friends.

"Any word yet?" she asked, stroking the crystal pendant hanging between her breasts. It was a habit she'd developed. Somehow touching the crystal gave her a measure of comfort.

"Nothing," Riley replied.

"Sheriff Monroe didn't find any signs of foul play," Millie added.

Cord pulled Savannah into the shelter of his body as a tremor coursed through her. She was glad for his unconditional support.

"What happened the last time y'all saw her?" Cord wanted to know.

Brock filled them in on Dakota's injury, and Tamara locking herself away in the cabin, music blaring. They'd all felt relieved when the music had been turned off, assuming she'd gotten over whatever had been bothering her and gone to bed.

No one had gone looking for her again until she had not surfaced by mid-afternoon the next day.

"It seems a little too coincidental both Dakota and Tamara disappeared around the same time," Millie said. "Those two have been dancing around each other since he got here."

Riley narrowed his stunning blue eyes at the cook. "There is nothing going on between them." He appeared angry at the mere suggestion.

Fisting her hands on her meaty hips, Millie stared the big man down, showing no fear of facing his wrath. "Then why was Tamara so hot and bothered any time Dakota showed the least bit of attention to Steph?"

As one, they all turned their gazes on Cord's younger sister.

Stephanie held up her hands in a defensive posture. "Hey, Dakota and I are just friends. He was teaching me about the horses. He's a very nice man, but I have no interest in him outside of friendship." She lowered her gaze briefly, then looked up at Riley in a shy manner from under thick lashes.

Interesting. Savannah fought a smile at seeing her sister-in-law's response to her friend. From the first moment she'd met the other woman she'd known there would be a connection between Steph and the prankster cowboy. Hopefully, Cord would allow things to develop instead of playing the overprotective big brother.

She was frustrated to be unable to get any sense about what was happening with Tamara, although it wasn't surprising. She'd never been able to see anything about her friend with her "second sight" abilities. Tamara was one of the few people able to keep her emotions hidden.

Sensing Zeke had something to say, she turned toward the shy man. The stress riding him over the situation was evident in his cloudy, cornflower blue eyes and mussed, sandy blond hair.

"Zeke? Talk to me, honey."

"We've all seen the way they look at each other, and the way Tamara acts whenever he's around." Looking down, Zeke dug the toe of his boot into the ground. "The scorching heat pouring off them when they watched Honey and Rowdy being mated was obvious."

Ah, she'd thought Dakota would have an impact on Tamara. It seemed logical to think they were likely together since they were both gone at the same time.

Her friends were all well aware of her abilities. Because of this, they tended to relax when she offered reassurance. Savannah had to hope today would be no different. Taking a moment to make eye contact with each of them seemed to help ease the thick tension.

After a brief, silent communication with her husband, Savannah wore a cheesy grin when he began speaking.

"So if all of you are playing amateur detective, standing around here fretting about that spitfire, who the hell is taking care of the ranch?"

Total and utter silence met the comment.

"That's what I figured," he said, sounding stern. "You're not being paid to lollygag around, chattering. I want y'all to get back to work."

Relief washed through her friends, allowing each to visibly relax. Knowing Cord was back and in charge gave them a measure of calm.

Guiding her with his hand at the small of her back, her husband ushered Savannah toward the house. "Come on, sugar. Let's go inside where you can relax before you start trying to reach out to Dakota."

His words made her heart swell. She'd never imagined finding such a wonderful, understanding man who accepted her abilities without question. The day he'd arrived on the ranch was one of the best days of her life.

She was disappointed her time alone with Cord had to end, but it felt good to be home. Being away from the ranch and her friends had left her antsy. They were such a big part of her life it didn't seem right not having them close.

When she was able to loosen up enough to attempt using her abilities, Savannah became certain both Dakota and Tamara were fine and having a good time together. She detected a connection growing between them, which lightened her heart. She hoped the easy-going man would have a positive effect on Tamara. Her inner voice told Savannah if anyone were able to reach her friend, it would be him.

For some reason, this knowledge didn't seem to reassure the cowboys. Jealousy emanated from all four of them. While they were very casual about their relationship with Tamara, she knew each of them cared a great deal for their friend. It would be interesting to see how all of this played out.

When they all returned to their normal activities, trying to act as if they weren't worried, a palpable air of expectancy hung over the entire ranch. Savannah overheard the cowboys plotting, and began to wonder if her friend would be able to handle the inevitable scene she'd face upon returning home. Jesse's words played through her head over and over.

"If that no-account Indian has Tamara, he's in for a world of hurt!"

Chapter Eleven

She must have dozed for a bit, slowly coming to awareness as Dakota lifted her into his arms and carried her across the canyon. He seemed to have no concern they were both naked, and she figured it didn't matter much since there was no one to see them other than animals.

With gentle care, he lowered them both into the hot spring. She relaxed in total comfort against his big body, enjoying the blissful warmth surrounding her. Mmm...glorious, but what met her gaze as she opened her eyes was even better.

Dakota.

A wide smile spread across her face and deep into the ravaged recesses of her soul. What a wonderful way to wake up, held cradled in her lover's embrace.

"Hi, handsome!"

"Hi yourself, gorgeous. How do you feel?" Dakota asked, a bright smile lighting up his dark eyes.

Even though it was warm outside, the steamy water brought wonderful relief to her sore muscles. Tamara purred with contentment. Actually purred. That had never happened before, yet it felt good. Right.

"Mmm...beyond fabulous."

Looking around, she took in their surroundings. It was a beautiful spot she would never have ventured to on her own. The enormity of what she was able to enjoy because of Dakota's tender caring washed over her. A whole new world lay at her fingertips. "This is incredible."

Dakota shifted her closer. He was in a relaxed, semi-sitting position with her draped across his lap and chest.

"It's a natural hot spring, and about the closest thing to a hot tub you're gonna find out here."

"I love it!" She snuggled against his broad chest, reveling in the sensations created by the gentle, warm waters caressing her tired body. However, after several minutes a slight frown creased her brow as she remembered everything that had happened.

THWAP!

She smacked his chest with her open hand. Dakota sat in stunned silence for only a moment before expressing his indignation at being hit for no apparent reason.

"Hey! What the hell did you do that for?"

What did he do? Ugh! The bastard had left her alone in the middle of the wilderness, which he knew scared the shit out of her, and caused her to suffer through those painful days of emotional upheaval. Past lessons learned flooded back with agonizing pain. There were good reasons she didn't form attachments, allow herself to feel. To love.

No matter how tender and loving Dakota was now, the pain would soon follow. He would try to take things from her she wasn't willing to give. Hell, he already had. He'd taken her very life and ripped it to shreds, opening her up to misery and heartache.

There was no way she would sit back and let this happen, allowing him to mold her into someone different, then pull the rug out from under her world once she became comfortable. She wouldn't know how to be this new person on her own.

Misery splintered through her, tearing apart scabs covering wounds which had never healed, taking her by surprise and splitting her wide open. The urge to turn from him, run in the opposite direction filled Tamara. Every muscle tensed with the readiness to spring into action. Shield herself and escape. These actions were as familiar as breathing and walking. This was how she survived.

Yet as she watched him from the corner of her eye, thoughts of what she'd be giving up came crashing down like a heavy weight against her chest, making it difficult to draw a breath. Dakota's quiet peace and assurance made her feel safe. His glorious, loving touch and heated, passion-filled kisses offered a beautiful haven. Burning love shone from his dark eyes. Thoughts of the way he'd touched her body with deep devotion and caring, the way he'd cherished her, made her feel like something precious and worthy of love.

What was she supposed to do, give up the person she'd become? Discard the difficult education she'd endured? An education which had taught her how to survive by keeping her heart protected? Risk the possibility of reliving bitter lessons she'd struggled to avoid repeating for so long? Could she give up all she was for the love and the connection she felt to this amazing man?

"I remembered I'm mad at you."

Dakota sat up a little straighter, no longer quite so relaxed. "Why, because I left you alone out here?" It was the only reason he was able to think of.

What about everything she'd learned since coming out here? Everything she'd felt and gone through. The demons of the past she'd fought and defeated, the tangible bond they'd created. Could she break the link with barely any care or concern, walk away from the first man to ever show her true understanding, compassion and affection? What of the casual way he'd walked away from her?

Tamara took a moment before answering then gazed at him with a hurt expression. "Well, there is that, too. I left you sleeping in my bed the other night while I went to dinner. When I came back, you were gone. No note, nothing. It royally pissed me off."

He hugged her closer as his dark expression became clouded, a storm brewed in his eyes. "I'm sorry if I hurt you, princess. I had no idea you'd be upset. The only thing on my mind when I woke up was getting into a hot shower, and rubbing some liniment on my aching hip."

THWAP!

She smacked his chest again.

"Hey! Now what the heck was that for?"

She thought about the horrible days and nights spent alone with her emotions, crying and screaming out for him, and how he'd stayed away. There were ways he may have eased her through the tortuous feelings assaulting her, yet leaving her alone had turned out to be the perfect catalyst to bring about true change and healing.

A slight smile curved her luscious lips when she answered. "For leaving me in the middle of nowhere."

"Ah. I'm sure you can see the wisdom in that, though."

She mumbled something noncommittal, but he wasn't going to let her skate around the issue. "Princess? Talk to me."

Tamara let out a deep sigh of frustration. "I understand why, and certainly can't argue with the results. It was just...frightening to wake up in the middle of the wilderness alone." A slight shudder coursed through her petite frame. "Dealing with so much bombarding me..."

Dakota's expression was contrite, but also firm in the belief he'd done the right thing. "Again, I'm sorry I hurt you, Tamara. You're not angry any longer, are you?"

Even if she were mad at him, the turbulent emotion wouldn't last for long. Dakota possessed such a giving and loving spirit, she knew his actions could never be malicious. Gradually, she released the tension, allowing her body to relax again in the shelter of his embrace and the warmth of the water.

Still, lingering doubts and unease flirted with her mind. If she permitted herself to love Dakota most of her freedom would disappear as the emotion chained her to him.

Allowing her hands to do the talking for her, Tamara trailed her manicured nails down his neck to caress his broad shoulders. She imagined those strong, capable shoulders bearing any burden, no matter how large.

The past few days, weeks even, seemed so surreal. The idea someone as patient and kind as Dakota existed was difficult to grasp. The fact he saw something in her worth loving...amazing.

Thinking back to her dream, she wondered what he thought of her body. Did he think her ribs stuck out too much and that she was too thin? Did he think she was a bad person because of her promiscuous lifestyle?

She was well aware people judged each other all the time, but in reality they were projecting their own perspective on another and not truly seeing the individual for who they were. How did Dakota see her?

Tears surged forward as too many new emotions assaulted her.

Escape. Run.

The urge to flee was overwhelming. She needed to get away from him, and began fighting against the arms holding her, which only resulted in Dakota tightening his grasp. He stared into her wide, frightened eyes.

"Talk to me, princess. What's going on in that pretty little head of yours?"

No. No more talk. She couldn't take it. A familiar rush of panic surged through her, increasing her struggles. Her heartbeat accelerated, chest tightening as the world closed in on her. All the while he spoke in soothing tones, which only increased her agitation.

"I won't let you run from this, from me, princess. It's not going to happen, so just relax."

Relax. How laughable. She wouldn't relax again until she got away from him and back to civilization. The insane man began nuzzling her neck, placing delicate kisses against her skin. His whispered words of love and reassurance made things worse.

"It's okay. I'm here and I'm not letting you go. I've got you."

And therein lay the problem. He had her held tight against his body when she needed to be anywhere else. No matter how hard she struggled to free herself, there was no escaping his greater strength. The bastard could keep her captive, force his intentions on her, and there was not a damn thing she'd be able to do about it. Echoes of the past repeating itself spread through Tamara. Memories of other men forcing things she didn't want scared the hell out of her.

"Let me go." Her voice was raspy, broken and sounded pathetic. Damn it. She would not be weak.

"I won't let you hide from my love." The statement was full of self-assurance.

He captured her thrashing arms, holding both wrists in one big hand, subduing her then lifting them both out of the spring, laying her down on the stone edge with her legs dangling into the water.

The anxiety had her in a tight grip now. Everything closed in on her and her only thought centered on fighting for her life. When she looked at him, she no longer saw the caring man who had come to mean so much to her. Instead she saw every slimy bastard who had ever forced something on her she didn't want.

Her arms were held stretched above her head, pinned to the hard surface while he used his body weight to hold her down. The only movement available to her was with her legs. Tamara kicked hard, accomplishing nothing but splashing water until she found an opening to mount her own attack.

Dakota made a move to encase her legs between his. If she let it happen she'd be well and truly caught, unable to defend herself. Pulling back one leg, she prepared to slam her knee into the vulnerable flesh between his legs, hoping to knock his balls all the way up into the beast's throat.

Somehow he anticipated the move. Reacting in time to keep her from scoring a fatal blow, he pinned her legs between his muscular thighs.

His mouth came down over hers with bruising force, seeking an entrance she was not willing to give. She clamped her teeth and lips together in a tight refusal. Tears streamed down her cheeks as he eased up and began tracing tender kisses over her lips.

His free hand cupped her breast, tweaking her nipple between his fingers and her traitorous body responded. Now he was really fighting unfair. Rough force she was accustomed to and capable of handling, but tenderness...

"I love you, Tamara. You can't drive me away. I won't let you run from me...from this...from us!"

Totally immobilized, she still struggled as much as possible. There was no way she'd lay back and let him have his way. He may rape her double-crossing body, but he would not take her mind.

How she'd gone from carefree, playful teasing one moment to fighting for her life the next, Tamara had no idea. The panic didn't give her the opportunity to stop and consider what was happening.

Dakota trailed soft kisses down her neck, lingering where her pulse pounded out of control, laving with his tongue. She felt her breasts swell, nipples elongating into hard beads, her body and mind fighting each other with violence equal to how she struggled against him. The more loving his words and tender his caress, the harder she battled.

"You own my heart. Returning it isn't a possibility. I'm all yours now, princess."

No one had ever made her feel so much. They were absolute perfection when together, beyond anything a man or woman could be as individuals. When joined they were everything—the very air, fertile ground, rocks and trees, water. They were life. The idea terrified and excited her at once.

"No. I don't want this." Her cry was full of desperation and she shook her head in denial of what she knew deep down inside.

His dark eyes captured her gaze. "Yes you do."

He merely continued, undeterred. When his mouth claimed her nipple, he gently sucked the turgid peak, creating a wet gush of arousal between her legs. Fuck! What the hell was wrong with her? How was she getting turned on by this unwanted attention?

"I don't want you," she sobbed.

The hand that had cupped her breast trailed down her abdomen. His fingers stroked over her mound before sliding lower to play over damp folds. Her blood heated, spiking her body's wanton desires.

"Don't lie to me, princess. You want me as much as I want you. I see the truth in your eyes. You're just afraid."

Damn him. Dakota was bound and determined to make her face what frightened her most, his love.

"Yes...no..." She didn't know what she wanted.

He licked and sucked at her, drawing almost her entire breast into the heat of his mouth as she broke down. Tamara was being pulled in different directions. She wanted him to stop. At the same time, she wanted him to continue more than she wanted her next breath. Her back arched, driving her closer to his mouth.

Her mind strove to retreat from the love she felt in every caress of lips and tongue. Pressing her nipple against the roof of his mouth, Dakota sucked with unbridled eagerness, stealing her fight and determination.

Oh, how she needed this man. He was like warm sunshine in the middle of a gloomy, winter day. A drink of crisp, clean water spilling down a parched throat. He held the key to her heart and salvation for her battered soul.

She didn't even realize her hands were free and she was no longer struggling against him, but instead struggling for more. Demanding everything. Her fingers probed everywhere she could reach.

Tamara was lost, mind and body at cross-purposes. With one heartbeat she tugged him closer and the next she pushed him away, fought for the freedom she no longer had. There would be no escaping this thing happening between them, sealing their fate.

Shoving his thick thighs between her legs, he spread her open. With one hand beneath each knee, he pressed her legs even further apart. She felt the silky head of his cock brush against her vulnerable opening, met by a gush of fluids raining down over their flesh. As much as she wanted him to drive into her pussy, stretching her to fit his thick cock, she wanted to bar him entrance, keep him at a distance.

No matter how she pushed and pulled or bucked and beat her fists against him, Dakota remained tender and gentle, showering her with his love. She was much better equipped to handle force, rage and lust. This caring, kindhearted assault on her senses was something she didn't know how to deal with.

The soft and insistent heaviness of his cock against her cunt was driving her insane. Her mind told her to pull away, while her body tried to increase the pressure and draw him inside. No matter what move she made, he countered it, keeping himself poised at her entrance.

"Dakota," she growled. "Just do it. Fuck me!"

He went absolutely quiet and still for a moment, those dark eyes holding her gaze. She saw the love and concern in the dark orbs, but refused to let her heart and emotions rule her actions.

"You want my cock, princess?" he growled.

"Yes," she pleaded, but what she felt went way beyond simple want, bordering on necessity.

She detected a multitude of emotions crossing his handsome face, understanding and love being the primary things she saw.

"I'll give you my cock, but will not fuck you. We'll make love. Always with love, Tamara."

With that said, he held her captive between the unyielding surfaces of the rock and his hard length, allowing her no chance to retreat. No option other than to take the pleasure he gave. No choice other than to accept the slow impalement of each thick inch of cock he pressed into her grasping pussy—the tender loving he was determined they share.

Endless inch after inch crowded into her, filling her to perfection until she had no idea where she ended and Dakota began. Still, he slowly drove his hard cock deeper, all the way to her heart and soul. When he was enveloped within her, body balls deep, he held still, staring into her eyes. Tamara writhed and bucked beneath him, trying to get him to move, but her efforts were futile.

Not until he wiped at the tears running in a steady stream down her cheeks did Tamara realize she was still crying. Some of his quiet words filtered through the sobs wracking her body.

"I love you, my princess, my heart. You can't drive me away. I will always be here." He then placed a soft kiss against her breast where her heart pounded in an erratic rhythm beneath her ribs.

She found it hard to believe he was still there with her, holding her in a loving embrace. Her entire body trembled as she tried to keep the overwhelming words of love surging within her soul from escaping through her lips.

The fight raging through Tamara broke as she whispered the three words refusing to be kept quiet any longer. The words came pouring from her heart.

"I love you." She spoke on a soft whisper as she finally set the emotions free, punctuated with a deep sigh of acceptance.

"Great Spirit. I love you so much, princess. It's going to be all right now."

When he started to thrust his cock in slow, easy strokes, a rush of joy seized Tamara. Her spirit soared, reaching out to Dakota, joining with this amazing man. Together they climbed, tangling their hearts and spirits together in ways she knew could not be undone.

She would never be alone again. Dakota would be by her side for the rest of her life.

He began chanting words in a language sounding older than time, speaking an ancient ritual binding them together, completing each steady thrust with the beautiful words she felt with every beat of her heart. They both exploded in blinding climax, flying into the heavens together on the wings of an eagle. The love and approval of the Great Spirit blessed their union, joining them for all time.

Chapter Twelve

Dakota's every thought and action over the past several days had gone into nurturing their love and strengthening the bond growing stronger between them. They'd been gone longer than he'd anticipated. By now it was likely the others had become concerned, but he knew Tamara would have to be sure of his feelings and devotion before they returned to the ranch to face her friends. She needed a great deal of reassurance and tenderness, and would have to realize he would never walk away.

Watching as she began to accept the kind of things most people took for granted was an amazing sight to behold. Things like casual conversation, having a lover ask her opinion or listen to her dreams. Even relating to a man in ways not involving sex was new to her. For Dakota, it was akin to watching a delicate bud unfurl its petals to the warm embrace of the sun as it bloomed with a new, radiant vitality.

They shared common tasks with joy—from preparing meals to cleaning up their living space. The fragile new vibrancy glowing from his spirit mate as she opened herself to what they created together brought him both hope and happiness.

After a lazy soak in the hot spring, they settled on a blanket at the base of a large pine tree to enjoy the warm breeze against their bare skin. She curled up in his lap like a kitten and fell asleep to the comforting cadence of his voice while he told her stories from his childhood.

Dakota still marveled at how such a huge spirit was contained within quite so small a package. His fingers looked huge against her cheek as he brushed a glossy mahogany lock behind her ear. It made him want to shelter and protect her from the world, even as he felt a sense of pride over how far she'd come in such a short time.

And when they made love...

Making love with Tamara was beyond anything he'd imagined. No matter how they came together—fast and fevered or slow and reverent—it was a total joining of spirits. The wildcat had the ability to heat his blood with a simple glance, bring his cock to attention with the slightest caress, and drive him to his knees with her intense sexual energy.

A frown pulled down the corners of her pouty lips and creased her forehead.

"You realize we have to go back, right?" Tamara's voice was raspy from sleep. "I have a business requiring my attention and you have a job."

She looked up at him, worry over returning to the real world apparent in her green eyes. He was worried too, but being able to read Tamara's emotions with such clarity in her expression lightened his heart. It showed how far she'd come, how much she had healed.

He didn't fool himself into thinking it would be easy to return to the ranch or that the battle had been won. Being back in the familiar atmosphere, old habits would try to reassert themselves and it would be tempting for her to slip into her old ways. And he predicted the cowboys would attempt to come between them, encouraging a return of the Tamara they knew.

"No matter how wonderful it is to laze around and play out here, we have to go back to the real world," she grumbled.

He understood her concerns, but there was no sense in worrying over what would happen in a future neither of them could control or stop from happening. Not when his sultry spirit mate lay curled against his body, her small hands beginning to wander, sending heat coursing through his veins.

"We'll handle it all together, but first..." Tamara gave him a smoldering look from under thick lashes. Her green eyes darkened with desire. Those beautiful eyes always captivated him, and her sexy glance made his cock stand up and pay attention as it thumped against her belly.

"I'm hungry," she mumbled against his chest. Her tongue snaked out to taste the muscular flesh cushioning her head. He felt her lips form a smile against his skin when he sucked in a sharp breath.

The hard edge of her nails sought out and teased his sensitive nipples, electric bolts of sensation racing down to his throbbing cock. Sharp shards of pleasure shot through him when her teeth scraped over his flesh. The warm, wet slide of her tongue against his nipples heated his blood to boiling. Tangling his fingers in her silky hair, Dakota held her mouth close to the rapid beating of his heart.

Her fingers played across his chest before moving lower. The warmth of her lips pressed sultry kisses over the ridges of his abdomen, blazing a heated path to join her fingers. He groaned when her nails raked through the dark curls covering his groin, wanting to demand she stop teasing and give him what he wanted, but enjoying the anticipation created from her playfulness.

Some thought must have tickled her funny bone because she giggled, the subtle vibration teasing his senses. Witnessing

Tamara learning to let go enough to have fun while making love was a heady aphrodisiac and a beautiful gift he treasured.

She gazed up at him often, gauging the reaction she elicited. He eased his grip on her hair, sweat breaking over his skin as she headed lower. He'd dreamed of seeing those full lips stretched around his cock, cheeks hollowed, sucking him deep into the warmth of her mouth. His princess was so beautiful, both inside and out.

Dakota's balls tightened and he was ready to climax from the seductive sight of her bent over his cock, mouth hovering over the bulbous head, back arched and heart-shaped ass thrust up into the air... Great Spirit, he considered himself to be a very lucky man.

One hand finally held his shaft close to the base, exerting firm pressure while the other cupped his balls and began a tortuous massage. Every muscle tightened and hot pleasure streaked through his groin. Tamara's pink tongue licked a wet path across her lips while she stared at his cock like it was a delicious treat she anticipated savoring. As they both watched, a pearly drop of pre-come beaded at the slit.

The slow and steady descent of her mouth created an ache within Dakota to thrust his hips to meet her halfway, but he didn't want to rush her. He wanted to relish his heightened senses being bombarded, delight in every touch, enjoy every sultry look, and melt under each lash of her tongue. Yet at her first hot swipe over the head of his cock, he moaned and bucked his hips. The extreme pleasure was both agonizing and heavenly.

She teased and tasted the entire plum-shaped head, then placed a tender kiss on his glans before tracing a scorching path around the prominent ridge. The hand gripping his shaft started to stroke him with small, slow movements, and a finger from the other hand began to slide along the shallow groove behind his sac, filling Dakota with the overpowering need for more.

It became obvious she was not unaffected by the sensual torture she created. Needing more stimulation of her own, Tamara dropped her hips down and began rocking her fiery pussy against his leg. Great Spirit, she was so wet. Her sweet cream coated his skin and filled the air with the musky scent of her desire.

He moaned her name as she licked and nibbled long, wet tracks from tip to root, taking great pleasure in discovering every ridge and vein of his silky, hot flesh. Giving into the ecstasy of her warm mouth enveloping his cock at long last, Dakota threw back his head and closed his eyes.

Her mouth sliding down over his cock engulfed him with a pure, absolute and utter bliss that might just drive him insane. The fingers wrapped around his shaft followed the movements of her lips as she began moving up and down. Rising up on his elbows, he watched his impassioned lover begin sucking his cock with sincere delight, eyes closed, cheeks hollowing while she struggled to take every inch, working to draw the very life right out of him.

"Damn, Tamara," he moaned. "You're killing me."

She looked at him from under heavy lids, her green eyes dark and determined. While her lips sucked and her head bobbed, her wicked tongue swirled over his shaft. Rolling his balls in one hand, she increased the pressure of her grip with the other.

It was all too much. No matter how much he desired to draw out the experience there was nothing he could do to delay his impending climax.

Giving himself over to gluttonous delight, Dakota began thrusting his hips, fucking her pretty mouth. Her muffled moans of satisfaction sent bolts of electric sensation streaking through his shaft to gather in his balls, which were drawn up tight and ready to explode.

"Fuck yeah. I'm going to come," he mumbled in warning.

Opening those beautiful eyes wide, Tamara watched him while sucking even harder, demanding her reward. Thrusting into her mouth one final time, he gave her everything, spilling his seed down her throat as she worked to swallow every drop. Once she had sucked him dry, she released his cock to lick her lips clean. A small trickle of pearly come ran from one corner of her swollen, reddened lips onto her chin.

Damn, he'd never seen a more beautiful sight.

Grabbing hold under her arms, he dragged her up his body, licking up the trail of his seed before sealing his mouth over hers, tasting his salty essence. He plunged his tongue into her mouth, drinking in the erotic flavors. Wrapping his arms around her, Dakota fought to slow down his racing heart and ease his rapid breathing.

Tamara was a writhing ball of sexual energy needing his attention. Her drenched pussy pressed against his still semi-hard cock, and she rocked her clit against him, hot cream dripping down over his balls.

The evidence of how much she'd enjoyed giving him head produced a fresh wave of arousal through his body, lengthening his cock once again. Tamara broke the kiss, pulling back and gasping for breath.

"Fuck me," she demanded.

Gripping his hips with her strong legs, she levered herself up his body until the tip of his cock found her soaked entrance. Wriggling her hand between them, she grasped his cock then slid down his length. She was so hot and ready, thick juices easing his way into her silken warmth.

"No, princess. Now, I will make love with you." He whispered the declaration in her ear then nibbled the soft lobe.

Her pussy spasmed and an inferno of liquid heat raced through her, gushing from her needy cunt. In this position, Tamara swore she felt every ridge and vein, felt him all the way up to her navel. She knew every wonderful texture and nuance of his gorgeous cock—by taste, touch and appearance.

Making love. It was a new concept, but one she decided was good. The magnitude of Dakota's love struck her, and she was taken by surprise with how alive he made her feel.

It was true. She was now living for the first time, cherishing every wonderful minute, all thanks to this amazing man she loved with complete and total devotion.

At first she began rocking her hips back and forth, unwilling to let even a mere inch of his cock slip from within her. Each gentle motion created a delightful friction against her clit, driving her need higher until she had no conscious choice. Her body took over, legs clasping against his hips, fingers clenching in his biceps, feral moans escaping her parted lips. Her pussy swelled, the walls gripping his cock tight, demanding more.

She became mindless with need, everything focused on cresting the mountain she climbed. Each thrust was more powerful, taking her higher, until Dakota shifted their positions to a small degree. The subtle change was all she'd needed. Now with each stroke her clit ground against his pelvis, creating shimmering sparks radiating out through her body. Her nipples pebbled to an almost painful hardness and every muscle tensed, preparing for an orgasm which took her by surprise with its intensity.

One moment she was struggling to reach the peak, the next she was flying through the heavens on the wings of a majestic eagle. She collapsed over Dakota, and he lifted her hips, thrusting into her one final time. He drove so far within her they melded into one seamless being.

Tamara buried her face in his chest, still holding on with the last of her strength as her muscles shook. Hot tears of joy and completion rolled across her cheeks, soaking into his flesh while her lover's hands soothed, stroking over her hair and back.

"Are you okay, princess?"

Concern was evident in Dakota's voice, but hell if she had an answer for his question. Was she okay? Over the past several days she had turned into someone quite different from the woman she'd been. Her whole reality and way of thinking had changed, reshaped. On top of everything else, she'd fallen in love and found fulfillment with one hell of an amazing man. Her body was in a state of absolute and total satiation, weak as a newborn kitten. Most likely she wouldn't be able to move anytime soon.

"Not sure," she mumbled into his pecs as her eyes grew heavy. The steady pulse of his heart beneath her ear relaxed her, and Tamara fell asleep again between one beat and the next.

Chapter Thirteen

Dakota enjoyed the peaceful ride back to the ranch with his spirit mate at his side. Even though he felt the tension thickening around Tamara, her face was suffused with a happy glow that gave him great joy. While she had always been a beautiful woman, with the bawdy attitude gone and her inner beauty shining through, she was breathtaking.

In his mind, he harbored some doubts about what would happen once they returned to the realities of ranch life. Although he'd helped her face down the past and come to terms with her life, Dakota wasn't sure she could be a one-man woman. Would she be able to let go of the cowboys and be content with only him? Maybe she would now expect him to join into their group games. While the idea was exciting, it was not what he wanted and needed. Tamara would be his alone or not at all.

She had told him she loved him, and while he believed the words came from her heart, their new love might not withstand the tests to come. He sent up a silent prayer to the Great Spirit, asking for the strength to face the coming challenges.

No, he would not allow himself to have negative thoughts. He would have faith in his spirit mate and their love. Everything would be fine.

Tamara's sweet voice broke his contemplative mood. "Would you like to come into town with me? I'd like to show you the Paperback Roundup."

Her beautiful face filled with a look of pride and there wasn't any way Dakota would've turned her down. "I'd love to see your bookstore. Once I check on the horses we can both shower and head into town. Wanna go to dinner somewhere nice afterwards?"

"Oooh, that would be wonderful." Her face lit up with happiness.

Dakota shifted in the saddle and leaned over to stroke her cheek in a tender caress. Great Spirit, how he loved pleasing this woman. She was everything he ever dreamed of finding in a mate and more. Being by her side brought him a wealth of pleasure.

Everything was quiet when they rode into the ranch yard. He helped Tamara down from the horse, steadying her until she got her balance. It had been a long ride and her legs were a bit wobbly at first. Hooking one arm around her waist, he pulled her against him and held her in a tight embrace, the other hand tangled in the hair at her nape. For several moments he stared into her green eyes, sharing a silent communication of love before claiming her mouth in a possessive kiss.

Her lips parted, and Dakota thrust his tongue into the cavern letting her taste explode through him. Tamara's hands slid up his chest and over his shoulders, clasping behind his neck. It had only been a matter of hours since they'd made love, but fiery want streaked through them creating a sensual energy. Breaking the heated kiss, he leaned back while they both caught their breath.

"Stop trying to distract me," he teased. "Go take a shower, princess. I'll meet you at the cabin in about an hour."

"Mmm...why don't you join me in the shower for a little afternoon delight first?" she propositioned, gracing him with a flirty smile.

Dakota shook his head with regret. "I've gotta take care of these horses, woman." Turning her away, he landed a playful swat on her gorgeous behind to get her moving. "The sooner you get going, the sooner we can play."

He didn't want her to see him limping or to realize the pain he suffered from riding, so he stood watching the gentle sway of her hips until she disappeared into the cabin.

After leading the horses into the barn, he stripped off the packs and saddles, then gave them a thorough grooming before checking on the other horses. One of the cowboys had recently cleaned the stables, and all the buckets were filled with water and feed. When he was satisfied everything was as it should be, he headed for the bunkhouse, anticipating the pleasure of a hot shower and then a good massage with some herbal cream for his sore hip.

Dropping his saddle bags onto his bunk, he headed directly for the shower. He'd unpack later. Dakota stripped off his clothes, adjusted the temperature to the hottest setting he could stand, and groaned with pleasure as the water pounded his sore muscles. Damn, did it ever feel good.

It wasn't until the water was abruptly cut off that Dakota realized he was no longer alone.

ᏣᏈᏌ

Standing in front of her closet, Tamara perused its contents, looking for the perfect outfit. After showering and drying her hair, she'd smoothed on a lotion scented with lavender, violets and musk, then put on peach lace panties and matching push-up bra. The lightly padded cups gave her breasts a lift, along with a fuller look.

Discarded outfits littered the bed by the time she finished debating what to wear, but she was finally satisfied with how she looked. The understated apricot halter dress conformed to her body, the flared hem falling to just below her knees. Coupled with a pair of high-heeled brown leather sandals, she looked adequately professional for the bookstore, yet sexy enough for an evening out. Perfect.

Merely being away from Dakota for this short amount of time made her ache for his touch and long for his kiss. Lord, what a mess she was becoming. They had not even been apart for an hour and already she was feeling needy and lonely.

She was putting the finishing touches on her make-up when she heard the cabin door. He was a bit early, which made it obvious he didn't like being separated any more than she did. Turning off the light before she left the bathroom, Tamara headed into the living room. "Well someone is impatient. Couldn't bear to be away from me, big boy?"

With a startled gasp, she stopped short and stared into a pair of apprehensive cornflower blue eyes.

"You know I hate being away from you, Tam."

"What's going on, Zeke?" Trepidation was obvious in her wavering voice.

For several heartbeats he stood looking down at where he twisted the toe of his boots in the area rug before ever making eye contact. "Look, I want you to know this was not my idea. I tried to stop them…"

Holding up a hand to silence him, she said, "Just tell me," with a fierce growl. "What have those fools done?"

Zeke remained quiet for several moments then motioned toward the couch. "Come and sit down, let's talk."

"Zeke," she said, raising her voice, "I don't want to sit and talk. Where is Dakota? What's going on?"

He sighed deeply. "Come and sit down, then I'll explain."

Fuck! She had to know what was going on and Zeke was going to be difficult. Every nerve ending in her body was zinging with energy, ready for action. She didn't want to sit and talk. But if she didn't comply with his request, Tamara would have no idea what to expect or where to look. He'd left her no choice.

Only when she perched on the edge of the couch, ready to take off in a flash, did he clasp her hands within his own and begin speaking.

"First of all, where the hell have you been?" he asked. He wore a concerned expression as he stared into her eyes, searching for answers. "You disappeared in the middle of the night without a word when it was obvious you were upset. We didn't know what to think."

Struggling to find some patience, Tamara took a deep breath. "Just tell me what the hell is going on, Zeke. Now!"

The stubborn man continued to stare into her eyes. "Not until you tell me what's happened over the past week."

She pulled her hands away and fisted them in her lap. "Fine," she grumbled. The sooner she told him, the sooner she'd figure out what was going on.

"Dakota took me out into the mountains for a break from the ranch and we...umm." She tried to find the right words for what she'd experienced, but how was she supposed to sum up such a powerful event in a few simple words? And until she knew what was going on, Tamara didn't want to say too much. Blurting out the words quickly, hoping to take any sting out of them, she simply said, "We connected."

Zeke nodded his head. "I had a feeling that would happen. Problem is the guys are kinda upset. We all thought something had happened to you. Even had the sheriff out here to investigate. And when they saw you two kissing..." He paused to collect his thoughts. "Well, they got all riled up."

Jumping up to her feet, she began pacing before the couch. "Where are they? What have they done to Dakota?"

Standing in front of her, Zeke held onto her arms, stilling her restless movements. "Answer one question first, Tam. How do you feel about Dakota?"

She stared into those sweet, caring blue eyes, not knowing where to start. How did she explain the things taking shape within her soul? "I don't have words to express what's going on, Zeke. He's so different from any man I've ever known. Dakota is amazing, patient, kind and gentle. I care about him—a lot. And I want to be with him all the time. I'm going crazy right now and we've only been away from each other for an hour. I..."

Zeke's perceptive words stopped her short. "You love him."

Tamara seemed to be happy, which was what mattered most to him. A bright smile spread across her full lips, lighting up her face. He didn't need to hear the admission, love filled her pretty eyes.

"Yes, I do. I am totally and completely head-over-heels in love with Dakota Blackhawk. Can you believe it?" she asked with a giggle. "It's absolutely wonderful and completely scary all at once."

He'd never seen her look so happy or heard her giggle like a schoolgirl. It was her unguarded, uncharacteristic response more than anything else telling him what he needed to know. Zeke pulled her in close and held her in a bone-crushing hug.

"I'm so happy for you, Tam, but we need to hurry. The guys are, er, having a little um...talk with Dakota."

"Shit, those morons!" She broke the embrace, grabbed Zeke's hand, and pulled him toward the door. "I'm gonna kick their asses."

CRSO

Her attention wavered and Savannah cursed under her breath as a sewing needle pricked her finger. She ignored the slight pain, her thoughts turning to events playing out on the ranch. She'd sensed Tamara and Dakota were back and the cowboys were up to no good. While certain whatever they were doing was a misguided attempt to protect their friend and lover, Savannah was afraid of tempers getting the better of the men. Sudden shouts coming from the ranch yard only justified her fears.

She raced down the stairs, abruptly skidding to a halt in the living room where several people looked to her for answers. Millie, Steph, Craig and Sandy Morton, along with their daughter Mandy, all appeared upset.

"What's goin' on?" Mandy asked.

"I heard the guys shouting," Steph added.

Millie had an aggravated expression on her face. "Those boys are up to somethin'."

The front door slammed open as Cord stormed into the room. Without a word he went directly to the gun cabinet and removed the shotgun. Turning to Savannah, he said, "You stay put." He punctuated the statement by pointing a finger at her chest.

Quicker than a flash of lightning, he was out the door and down the porch steps. Like hell if she was going to stand there and do nothing. She glanced at the others briefly.

"Be careful, ya hear," Millie said. "Those boys are wound tight and loaded for bear."

Steph looked frightened, but ready to help. Savannah grabbed her arm and the two of them ran out of the house hot on Cord's heels. He'd already made it to the bunkhouse before they made it through the door. Angry shouts echoed around the yard when he ducked inside, the gun resting over one arm and pointing to the side.

The two women clamored up the steps and through the doorway in time to hear Cord's comments.

"Just what the hell do you think you're doing?"

Racing into the room, Savannah was so stunned by the sight greeting them she almost ran right into Cord's back. At the far end of the room, Dakota was tied up between the ends of two bunk beds, arms and legs stretched wide. Water dripped off his naked body to puddle on the floor beneath him, long black hair clinging to his face and shoulders. He cringed when he saw her and Steph enter the room.

Cord turned on them before either woman had a chance to fully take in the scene. "I told you to stay put," he growled in an angry tone. He grabbed each of them by an arm and dragged them outside as Zeke and Tamara were making their way across the yard.

Tamara stopped next to Savannah. "What the hell have they done?" she asked. The murderous look on her face told Savannah everything she needed to know about the past week. Tamara was in love.

Looking at them all pointedly, Cord threatened severe punishment if anyone moved from the spot. Then he turned and pushed Zeke in front of him and into the bunkhouse, slamming the door shut behind them.

Savannah turned and hugged her friend tight, laughing over the sounds of a loud tirade that followed.

"Why the hell you married such a bossy cowboy is beyond me!" Tamara stomped her foot in agitation.

Pulling back, they looked at each other and burst out laughing.

"Are you okay, Tam?" Savannah asked the question, but didn't wait for an answer. "You look wonderful!"

Steph stared for a moment before commenting. "You look like a completely different person. What happened?"

Before Tamara formed a response they all turned toward the bunkhouse, startled out of their reunion by the sound of wood furniture splintering.

"I'll kill every one of those boys if they hurt Dakota," Tamara growled. She sounded like a protective she-wolf.

Savannah was thrilled to see the changes in her friend. The love and happiness surrounding Tamara were palpable.

"Well, um..." Steph started to explain the scene they had walked in on, but they all fell silent when the door busted open and Jesse stormed down the steps, not stopping until he stood toe-to-toe with Tamara. The man looked mad enough to spit. His brown hair stood in wild disarray and his amber eyes were filled with fire.

Riley, Brock, Zeke and Cord were all right behind him, each man looking equally disheveled.

"Don't you ever scare us like that again," Jesse hollered at her. "You have no idea how worried we were."

Brock stepped up next to Jesse and slowly looked Tamara over from the top of her head all the way to the heels of her shoes. Without a word, he pulled her into a fierce but brief hug before releasing her. "Is he telling the truth?" His tone was low and dangerous.

Tamara took her time, making eye contact with each of the cowboys, one thin eyebrow arched high. "Depends on what he told you."

Chapter Fourteen

Dakota called out to her and Tamara reacted on pure gut instinct. She ran up the stairs and into the bunkhouse only to stop dead in her tracks, jaw hanging wide open. She heard the others moving into the room behind her, but all of her focus remained on him. Tied up, naked and vulnerable, he still radiated an air of strength and calm, which reached out and wrapped around her in a comforting embrace.

He was so beautiful. Her gaze drifted over his dark skin taking in every masculine plane and angle. The way his arms were positioned showed off the strong muscles of his biceps to perfection. When his arm twitched slightly, his pecs tightened and his abdominal muscles rippled.

Even flaccid, his cock was an impressive sight, the base surrounded by a nest of dark hair, the thick shaft extending along the crease of his hip. The power contained in his solid thighs made her shiver in anticipation of a long, hard ride all the way to heaven.

Her body heated and she got wet from only looking at him. They would definitely have to reenact this scene later, without all their friends.

Something miraculous happened when their eyes met. The million or more fragmented pieces of her soul all shifted, coalesced and fell into place, creating a new whole from the

Nicole Austin

fractured past. Everything became clear, sharply focused. All the remaining weight of the past lifted away, leaving her with a light heart and calm spirit. With a serenity she'd never before possessed, not even for a minute, Tamara began to speak what was in her heart as she moved around the room.

From a nearby cabinet she retrieved a towel. Moving to Dakota, she wrapped it around his hips, covering his nudity from the others who'd followed her into the bunkhouse. Never looking away from him, she finally answered Brock's question.

"Yes, he told you the truth." She trailed her fingers in a loving caress over the angle of his jaw before moving to his side to begin loosening the bindings.

"I didn't go into the mountains of my own free will. Dakota picked me up, drunk and passed out. He carried me off into the night then left me alone in a canyon."

The gasps from her friends didn't stop Tamara from telling her story. They'd wanted to know, after all. "He didn't do it to be cruel, as I first suspected, but to help me make peace with myself and my past."

No one said a word or moved as she took her time working the knots in the rope free. Hell, she didn't think anyone even breathed while she revealed the depth of the life-altering events.

"As you can imagine, I was in quite a state when I woke and realized he'd left me out there alone. I screamed, threw a temper tantrum, cried and raged. At length, I thought about my life, finally coming to terms with my past and who I'd become, not liking the woman I faced down."

Dakota adjusted his stance on his freed legs, supporting his body while she continued to work on his bonds. He didn't interrupt, allowing her to tell the story in her own way. Pride filled his expression as he watched her handle the awkward

178

situation and allay her friends' fears. She'd come such a long way.

"I gave up my guilt, fear and anger over the past, came to terms with who I am, and found a place in my heart for love." She stroked her hands over every inch of flesh and continued removing the ropes until he was free, taking special care in areas where his skin was abraded.

Silent and still, Dakota stared into her eyes while she spoke, providing strength, unconditional support, and love.

"When we made the ride back here, I left behind the hurt to begin a new life with the man I love." They held each other in a warm embrace for a moment before she turned her attention to the group who had gathered. These were her friends, people who had stood by her, yet she'd never given them anything in return. It was time for a change.

The only ones not present were her newest friends, Millie, Craig and Sandy Morton, and their daughter Mandy. Later on she'd express her feelings to them.

Dakota moved up behind her, placing his hands on her shoulders in a silent offering of love she was glad to have. She looked over each of the stunned, speechless people gathered before her, then moved forward.

She stood before Zeke and Riley, who both reached out for her, holding her in a warm embrace. "Thank you for being my friends."

When they released her, she moved to stand before Cord and Savannah. "Thank you for being an example of the kind of love possible between a man and woman." The three of them shared a long hug.

Moving to stand before Brock and Jesse, she said, "And thanks for being my family."

After hugging the two men, she returned to stand with Dakota. Looking into those dark, caring eyes, she said, "I love you."

Before she knew what had happened they were all there, surrounding her with love and warmth, each talking a mile a minute in an attempt to be heard above the others. Tears filled her eyes knowing she had so many wonderful people in her life. Their easy acceptance was more than she'd hoped for, and a welcome surprise.

She was no longer the lost puzzle piece. Tamara had finally found right where she belonged. The picture solidified in her mind, revealing their ranch family gathered together, each looking happy and content.

CRSO

By the time they made it to town the sun was beginning to set, casting a brilliant show of deep, vibrant colors across the night sky. With their fingers interlocked, they walked along the sidewalk toward the bookstore, enjoying the beautiful night and quiet companionship.

Dakota was not surprised by the reaction of the older couple approaching from the opposite direction. All his life, he'd faced prejudice and fear, but Tamara was not accustomed to such blatant displays of intolerance. Although he sensed her tension and rising anger, he didn't predict her volatile reaction to their being shunned.

The couple stepped off the sidewalk into the grass as they neared, to avoid coming close to the Indian and his tainted white girl. Their distaste was written clear as day in their expressions.

Pulling him along using a physical strength that took him by surprise, Tamara stepped right in front of the pair. "Do you have a problem?" she spit out.

The wife remained silent and somewhat behind her husband who was emboldened by his hatred. "It's not me with the problem, missy. My wife isn't a half-breed, and my children don't have tainted blood like yours will."

Visible tremors shook Tamara's small body. The shock of his statement left her speechless. But not for long.

"You disgusting, narrow-minded bigot. I sure hope you didn't teach your children to be so hateful. This land belonged to the Native American people before ignorant, self-righteous people like you decided they were somehow inferior because of their differences. And it was this proud race you deem inferior who acted with grace in the face of having their very way of life destroyed by assholes like you."

Wow! You go, spitfire. An overwhelming surge of pride filled him from watching his princess put on such a vehement defense.

Dakota wished the couple a pleasant evening and ushered Tamara away from the heated confrontation. He was proud to be loved by a spirit mate who would stand against injustice and fight to protect those she cared about, but wanted to end the confrontation. He'd been truly blessed the day he'd found his princess.

She launched into a spirited diatribe as they continued their walk to Paperback Roundup. Frustration, hurt and disbelief shook her, each word filling her rant with a new energy and passion. Great Spirit, he loved the wildcat.

He loved every facet of his fierce princess from the bawdy, badass attitude to the vulnerable, hurt woman she tried so hard to hide from the world. All he had to do was look at Tamara or even just think of her to bring powerful emotion welling up within his heart.

He'd never imagined how intense the experience of having a spirit mate, or feeling this way for another person, would be. His happiness was wrapped up in her own. It was a frightening and daunting concept, but also wondrous and amazing—something he'd longed to feel all his life.

No sooner had they entered the store than he captured her in a strong clinch. Tamara's resistance and anger melted away under the gentle pressure of his lips. He placed butterfly kisses over the angry lines marring her forehead, against her tightly closed eyelids, then along her nose and cheeks before brushing her quivering lips.

She opened for him with a deep sigh. Dakota put all of the powerful emotions he felt into the mating of their mouths. What started as a slow, tender joining became fueled with overwhelming desire and passion. The angry tension was quick to melt away, replaced with ferocious sexual energy.

Her hands slid up his arms, fingernails gripping his biceps almost to the point of pain while she consumed him. Their bodies curved into each other, getting as close as possible with only their clothing coming in between. Her leg slid over his, and Dakota's hand clasped under her thigh, raising the limb to his hip.

He had no idea how many times the guy behind the counter cleared his throat before the sound filtered through the frenzied sensual heat enveloping them. Letting her leg slide back down, he broke the kiss and looked up into the smiling face of a man he liked on first sight.

Tamara looked dazed. Her eyes were darkened with desire and heavy lidded. It took a few moments for her to collect herself enough to make introductions. He was thankful, for her sake; there were no customers in the store to witness their shameless display of lust. Not that it would have bothered him. Instinct told him she'd be upset for her patrons to glimpse a slip in her professional demeanor though.

Letting the pride he felt over what his princess had accomplished with the store show in his expression, Dakota paid close attention as she showed him around. Overall it was a comfortable place to shop or sit and discuss the latest book releases with a friend over coffee. The wide selection of books offered something for every taste.

While she spent some time going over business details with the manager, he looked over the offerings, catching her watching him as he moved around the store. Finding a magazine to page through, he sat in a comfortable chair, his mind on the past few weeks and the future.

He knew Tamara didn't understand the significance of the words he'd spoken when their spirits joined out at his camp in the mountains. Before long he would have to explain the ceremony, and let her know according to the beliefs of the Cheyenne culture they were married. Then it would be time to tell his family.

Thinking about his family warmed his heart, but also worried him. How would his spirit mate react to the outgoing, eclectic group?

Dakota was so lost in thought he'd not even realized they'd locked up the store for the night, dimmed the lights, and the manager had retired to his apartment upstairs. Not until she came up behind him, whispering in his ear. Her breath warmed his neck and sent shimmering awareness throughout his body.

"I've always had this fantasy about closing up one night and finding a handsome stranger waiting in the darkness."

He closed the magazine, setting it on a nearby table, waiting to hear the rest of her fantasy. She didn't disappoint.

"The attraction is immediate, making my abdomen clench. I can feel my blood heat, rushing to my cunt where my labia swell and become slick with my cream. I want the handsome stranger. The look of desire in his eyes lets me know he wants me too."

The light brush of her fingernails over his shoulders combined with the slow seduction of her husky voice sharing a secret desire had his cock hard and ready. He wanted to reach down and set it free from the confinement of his jeans, but this was her show.

Moving around the chair, she took his hands, encouraging him to stand before backing away slightly.

"We play a game of cat and mouse, advance and retreat, as without word we circle around each other, assessing actions and reactions."

As she spoke they began to act out the enticing scene she described. Electricity seemed to crackle in the air around them as hunger built.

"I can tell from the way he stalks me, this man is a dominant predator determined to possess me, take me in a primitive joining. His body is powerful, so much stronger than my own. Images of him stripping off my clothes, taking me with a violent need are making me burn. It's exactly what I want from him. No words or expectations, only animalistic lust unleashed—hard, deep, feral fucking."

Damn, he easily pictured it too. While very different from his nature, Dakota imagined what it would be like to release the inner beast and act solely on impulse. He watched Tamara reach for the halter tie at her nape, then drag the soft material over her body with a slow deliberation, making him yearn to glimpse each inch of smooth, soft flesh. She was so beautiful it blew his mind.

Following her lead, he began to unbutton his shirt, matching the slow, tortuous pace she set. They still circled around each other, looking for any opening which might be exploited to their advantage.

"My mind tells me I have to be strong, not giving an inch, but my body wants to be weak and allow his dominance. I'm burning up with the need to be fucked. My pussy clenches, and hot juices slide down the sensitive walls to coat my thighs."

The opportunity came when she stopped moving, bending over to unbuckle the straps on her shoes. Without thought, Dakota sprung, determined to give her what she wanted, finish what she'd started. He'd gone into the role she established with ease, mind and body turning to a savagery he'd never known, yet adapted to without question.

Not once did he think about her being weak or fragile as he rushed forward, tackling her to the floor beneath him. Blind need took over and he followed his instincts and the fantasy she'd spun. With rough hands he flipped her over, putting her on her hands and knees while pushing the dress up past her hips so it bunched around her waist, baring her to his devouring gaze.

"Oh, yes," she panted. "Take me."

With one hand he forced her shoulders down. The fingers of the other seized the silky material of her panties, ripping them from her body. Using his knees, he spread her legs, wanting to roar at the sight of her swollen pink lips covered with her juices. The smell of musky arousal filled his lungs with each breath he took.

She glanced over her shoulder and tried to reach for him. Dakota grabbed her wrists, restraining both at the small of her back in one of his hands, driving her cheek to the floor. One small corner of his mind balked at his brutal treatment of the woman he loved, but she'd unleashed something he was unable to simply turn off. Not without satisfying the beast raging inside him.

Not even the hounds of hell would prevent him from plunging into her at this point. Nothing except her telling him no and that wasn't the words he heard rolling off her tongue.

"Oh, yes," she cried.

Her soft whimpers and pleas only made him more mindless. One thought kept playing through his mind in an endless loop. Fuckherfuckherfuckher.

The raspy sound of his zipper was loud in the quiet store, making her tremble beneath him. He freed his throbbing cock, and without preparing her in any way, slammed every inch as deep into her clenching pussy as it would go.

She was wet and ready, taking him with ease, her thick cream paving the way. Dakota never paused, merely began hammering her with his shaft, letting the blinding passion she'd provoked take over.

Tamara screamed and thrashed beneath him, face pressed against the carpet. Everything he was had narrowed down to his cock. That's all there was, his erection shafting her, taking what was his. He gave her exactly what she'd said she wanted, hard and fast primal fucking.

Never in his life had he worried about his own pleasure first or allowed himself release before ensuring his partner found pleasure, but his own climax was the only thing entering his mind now. He pounded into her so hard they moved forward with each punishing thrust, flesh slapping against flesh. It was a pretty safe bet she'd end up with some rug burn on her knees and shoulders, maybe even her cheek.

His climax took him by surprise, intense sensations grabbing him by the balls, sending molten-hot jets of come through his cock, filling her with his essence. She tightened around him, strong muscles grasping at his pulsing shaft. She screamed his name as her orgasm crested, drawing out his pleasure.

His princess collapsed in sated exhaustion and Dakota followed her down to the floor, rolling them onto their sides and curving his body around hers. They lay panting, slow to recover from the frantic coupling.

A small glimmer of guilt pricked at his conscience over the harsh way he'd taken her, but it had been glorious to let go with his mate.

As if sensing his thoughts she said, "Damn...that was good."

Pulling her even closer against him, Dakota let his hands stroke over her silky skin. So many feelings were rushing through him. He was overwhelmed and yet content to just hold his spirit mate within the shelter of his body.

She was his now. It was his responsibility to make sure she was happy, comfortable, safe and loved. He'd make sure she never lacked for anything she desired. He was serious about his responsibility and would do everything possible to be everything she needed for the rest of their lives.

Chapter Fifteen

Dakota's family had been anxious to meet his spirit mate, but he didn't feel she was ready. He wasn't worried about them liking each other, but something kept him from allowing it to happen right now. He held the family off, explaining it was not possible for the two of them to leave Montana before Wyatt Bodine's trial was completed. Savannah needed Tamara there with her in court each day for moral support. When the trial ended, he'd had to scramble for more excuses.

What a tremendous relief it was for everyone when the long ordeal was over and the judge put the sociopath away where he'd be prevented from harming anyone for a long time.

Working in the corral with one of the horses, Dakota kept mulling over something Savannah had said at breakfast. They'd been discussing his work with the animals when she began talking in riddles. He got the sense she was trying to clue him in to something by telling him to watch out for his tribe, and saying his filly would bolt when overwhelmed.

It didn't make any sense. He didn't have a tribe on the ranch, unless she was talking about the other cowboys, warning him they were plotting something. And the horse they'd been talking about—the filly he was working with now—had the most serene disposition of any he'd ever worked with.

Taking a look around the yard, he noted everything was as peaceful as it had been since the drama of their return from the mountains. The cowboys were all busy with their individual work for the day. He was the only one who seemed to be fidgety and tense.

The sound of a screen door smacking against its frame drew his attention to the main house where Steph now stood on the porch, stretching lazily. Tamara and Savannah were busy inside decorating the nursery. The two women had become much closer since his princess had learned to open up and begin trusting her friends. They had dragged Sandy in there to help, too, attempting to forge a bond with their newest friend.

When she spotted him, Steph walked over to the corral and leaned against the fence in a lazy posture. "I can't stand being inside for another minute," she complained. "There's no way to get any work done when they're constantly interrupting to show me paint colors, wallpaper samples, and catalogues of crib bedding. Ugh!" She groaned in frustration. "And Savannah keeps coming into the room every five minutes to peer out the window into the yard like she's waiting for something."

Hmm...that last bit was interesting. What had she envisioned would happen? He knew somehow it involved him, but still had not figured out her cryptic words from earlier.

Mandy came strolling up to the corral at a slow pace as they stood talking. It was unusual to witness the girl, who was normally a flurry of activity, looking so lethargic.

Noticing the same thing, Steph said, "What is up with everyone today?"

He didn't get a chance to respond as they all turned to watch a convoy of vehicles kicking up a thick cloud of dust on the ranch drive. Dakota figured he was about to find out what Savannah had been waiting for all day. It surprised him she hadn't appeared outside yet, but then he saw her silhouette in an upstairs window.

The unexpected approaching vehicles captured everyone's attention. Before long he was surrounded by his friends. Everyone was there with the exception of the three women, which made Dakota a bit suspicious.

Even before the assortment of cars and trucks had come to a complete stop, people were pouring out the doors and Savannah's words began to make sense. His family had lost their patience and made the trip from Colorado to meet his spirit mate. He groaned when he saw no one had been left behind. Every aunt, uncle, cousin and even a few close family friends had made the trip to the ranch. Great.

Seeing Steph standing close to him, the only woman among the gathered group, his family jumped to the assumption she must be the one. They rushed forward, all talking at once, and Steph was drawn into their ranks. He tried to get a word in above all the commotion, but it was too late. Steph was being passed from one person to another to be hugged and kissed as she was accepted into the fold. Poor Steph looked overwhelmed and frazzled, trying to figure out why she was being welcomed into his family as though she were a member.

It didn't take long before they moved on to his friends, pulling them into the pandemonium. His only option was to climb over the corral fence and accept the warm greetings and congratulations. When things began to settle down, he held up his hand to get their attention and informed his family Steph was a friend, not his spirit mate. Catching on to the misunderstanding and eager to get their attention focused somewhere, anywhere else, Steph pointed to the porch where Sandy, Savannah and Tamara had appeared, standing a safe distance away to observe what was happening.

"Tamara is Dakota's girlfriend, not me," Steph stated.

Making sure they would not be drawn into the rush of people headed their direction, Savannah and Sandy stepped back, leaving Tamara to face the crowd alone. Their actions singled her out.

If there was any way humanly possible for Dakota to have reached her first, he would have kept his family from overwhelming his princess, but there was nothing he could do. Tamara looked shell-shocked as they descended upon her and she experienced the force of nature that was his family for the first time. A panicked expression crossed her face as his female relatives began talking about bonding ceremonies and sewing a wedding quilt.

Cord clapped Dakota on the back. "Dang. Quite the tribe you've got there." The other men all chuckled, but he only heard Savannah's words rolling through his mind.

"Your filly will bolt when the tribe overwhelms her."

And that's exactly what Tamara did. It made him think of the movie about the woman who always got scared when walking down the aisle at her weddings and would run away.

As soon as she managed to untangle herself from his family, she took off through the screen door. Only seconds after it slapped shut, he saw her run around the back corner of the house, headed straight for the Jeep. She was locked safely inside and headed down the drive before he reached her.

CRSO

Holy shit! Tamara had no idea what had happened. One minute Savannah was dragging her out onto the porch to see who had come to visit, and the next she was mobbed by a pack of way-too-friendly people who were related in various ways to Dakota.

She'd been so unprepared for the boisterous, affectionate group. Every one of them had felt the need to touch or embrace her in some way. Did they have no clue what personal space was?

All their rowdy attention had driven her right into a panicked state. Her throat had closed up, chest tightening until she was unable to breathe. She'd come close to clawing at her throat to get the oxygen she required. Then they'd started talking about ceremonies and tradition and her stomach had turned into a heavy rock, the sour taste of bile rising in her throat.

The only thing she'd been able to focus on was to escape or perish—save herself. She imagined what Dakota and her friends must think, but it was plain and simple, she'd had to get out of there.

Crap! She'd made a fool out of herself in front of his entire family, embarrassed both of them, and left him holding the bag. He was probably madder than hell.

At first she drove with no destination in mind, but then ended up going to the one place where she controlled everything, Paperback Roundup. If she'd known the way out to the deserted canyon in the mountains, she might have gone out where no one would bother her. At the store, there were customers and staff to deal with, although she could lock the office door and hide out in the safe haven.

It was exactly what she did, too. She hid in her office like a coward. Right up until the time someone started pounding against the door a few hours later, demanding entrance.

"It's only me, princess. Open up." Hearing Dakota's deep voice helped ease her jumbled emotions only marginally. She took her time walking to the door, taking deep breaths, readying herself to see the recrimination and anger in his dark eyes.

No sooner did she turn the door knob than he shocked the hell out of her by grabbing her in a fierce hug and holding her within the shelter of his strong arms. After tucking her head under his chin, he spoke and the words melted her heart.

"Are you all right, Tamara? I'm so sorry. They didn't tell me they were coming." Easing back, he tilted her chin up, his expression full of remorse. "I know they can be overwhelming, but they were all so anxious to meet you."

She felt incapable of forming actual words, but knew she had to say something. "You're not mad?" she managed to get out.

The look on her face hurt Dakota, making him feel like a fist clenched around his heart. It was the look of a bewildered child who didn't understand she had his unconditional love and devotion. Mad? He wasn't mad she'd run from the daunting ordeal of meeting his well-meaning but over-exuberant family.

"Of course I'm not mad, princess. I love my crazy family, but you will always come first."

He caught the tear rolling down her cheek on his finger, then picked her up and carried her over to the desk, kicking the door closed behind them. With one swoop of his arm, Dakota cleared off the desktop and laid her down.

"It almost killed me seeing how shaken you were and I couldn't get to you."

With tender, gentle hands, he pulled her shirt over her head and tossed it to the side, then did the same with her bra, shoes, jeans and panties. Keeping his eyes locked on her, he took his time removing his own clothing.

Not an inch of her skin was left untouched or untasted before he moved between her widespread legs. She was pleading by the time the head of his cock rested against her slick, swollen folds.

Any lingering doubts and insecurities she had were swept away by the intense look of devotion in his dark eyes. Tamara had found something in Dakota she'd never even dared to dream or hope would be part of her life. He'd helped her to heal the scars of a painful past, and begin envisioning a beautiful future. One in which she would never be alone.

He made love to her with breath-stealing thoroughness then vowed they would always be side-by-side, making their way together as equal partners, facing each day with love.

Epilogue

Denver, Colorado

Jesse Powers stared out the sliding glass doors but saw nothing.

Leaving his friends and normal way of life behind in Montana to pursue a dream had seemed an easy decision. A real no brainer, he'd thought. He would stand on his own two feet and make it in a completely foreign environment without a hitch.

Yeah, right. Lord, he had so much to learn.

What did he think he was doing smack dab in the middle of the Denver business jungle? He was like a fish out of water, floundering in an attempt to survive without a snowball's chance in hell of actually doing so.

Jesse was a good ole country boy who belonged in worn denim and dusty boots, not custom-tailored suits, fancy spit-shined leather shoes, tight-collared shirts, and ties that came close to choking him. He had no business trying to order something edible from the indecipherable menus in elegant frou-frou restaurants while rubbing elbows with the serious movers and shakers.

Even though they treated him with the utmost respect while vying for the pleasure of having him pay for their overpriced services, he sensed an undercurrent of disdain. They weren't buying the act. He wasn't fooling anyone, least of all himself.

What he wouldn't give to be back at the ranch. He pictured himself sitting in the bunkhouse with his feet propped up on the old wooden table and a longneck beer in his hand, shooting the shit with the guys. Instead he stood here, staring out into space as a crew of movers set up expensive rented furniture he didn't even like in a highfalutin' apartment he despised.

If things went well here, he would be able to return to the ranch and manage his business without ever having to leave the comfort of home. All he had to do was manage to navigate these uncharted waters, avoid the sharks, and then hightail it back to the Shooting Star and his friends.

Simple, right? He'd thought so.

Problem was he'd never imagined how alone and out of place he would feel. In the middle of endless, sleepless nights, Jesse would find himself returning to the website he'd helped Steph design for the ranch's horse breeding program. He'd stare with overwhelming longing at the pictures of his home, listening to Savannah's familiar voice on the recorded message over and over. It wasn't anywhere close to being there, but did provide a small measure of relief.

As he was about to turn away, a flash of color and movement in the building across the way caught his eye. Maybe this apartment wasn't so bad after all. It afforded him an unobstructed view into the bedroom of a goddess. Fuck yeah!

The sultry redhead was unbuttoning a white blouse as she walked into the room looking all hot and bothered. Without closing the blinds over the sliding glass doors, she walked closer. Standing facing him, she dropped the blouse into a silky puddle at her feet then slid down the zipper of a bronze mini-skirt, and it too joined the discarded top.

Fuck. He'd never seen anyone half as gorgeous as the beautiful temptress. Jesse felt kind of sleazy for watching, but he wasn't about to tear his eyes away from the fiery woman. There was something about her, other than being almost naked, which captivated him.

She stood wearing the sheerest pink bra and panties, which hid nothing from his hot gaze. He clearly saw the dark circle of her areolas topping the most amazing set of tits. Aw, Gawd. He could even detect a deep red patch of hair between the long legs that went on forever. A garter belt spanned her narrow waist, holding silk stockings in place.

Jesse imagined removing her panties with his teeth, then bending her over the footboard of the bed. The spiked heels she wore would put her at the perfect height to be taken from behind. Her silk stockings would brush against his legs while his hard cock slammed into the tight grip of her pussy.

Or better yet, he would take her against the wall, those luscious legs wrapped around his body, pulling him deep into the saddle created between her thighs just for him. He'd ride her hard for hours until they were covered with sweat and exhausted.

Hell yeah! What a sweet ride she would be.

Even from the distance between them, he noticed her nipples puckered in invitation, pressing against the thin covering. She stood with her head hanging back, arms held out and the flow of air from the ceiling vent ruffling the long, thick mass of dark red hair over her creamy skin. Damn, how his fingers ached to slide over her bare skin.

So beautiful and confident. She appeared to be secure and comfortable with her body, abandoning herself to the hedonistic pleasure of the cold air rushing over bare flesh.

His cock hardened and felt like it was ready to bust right through the thick denim jeans. With deft fingers he opened the button, relieving some of the constriction, and stroked over the thick ridge while observing the ethereal angel across the way.

She looked like a classy woman. Someone who belonged on the arm of a powerful, successful business man. Absolutely way too fine for a simple cowboy. He'd never have a woman like her, but wouldn't pass up this chance to witness an unguarded moment with such a ravishing beauty.

Jesse wondered what she was like. Did she realize how gorgeous she was and walk with her nose high in the air, ignoring the common people around her? Did she spend her nights being wined and dined by the crème de la crème of society? Maybe she was a little more down to earth. He sure hoped so.

As if she sensed his intense scrutiny, the seductive vixen slowly raised her head and looked right at him. Jesse was trapped, drowning in the most breathtaking pair of emerald green eyes. His mystery woman seemed unconcerned to be standing before him in her current state of undress. For the length of several heartbeats her gaze wandered his body with clear interest, then she smiled and he was lost. Plump, rosy lips spread wide to reveal a dazzling flash of white teeth and her whole face lit up.

Making no attempt to cover herself, the seductress made a slow turn on her heel and strolled away with the casual air of someone taking a walk in a quiet park.

He had no idea how long he stared into her bedroom, stroking his dick, wondering how to get a high-class broad like her on his arm and in his life. All Jesse knew was that he desired the sexy siren. Somehow, someway, he'd figure out how to capture the woman who'd just stolen his heart.

About the Author

To learn more about Nicole Austin, please visit www.nicoleaustin.net. Send an email to Nicole at nicoleaustinsizzles@yahoo.com or sign up for her Yahoo! group to join in the fun with other readers as well as Nicole! http://groups.yahoo.com/group/TandA_FantasyPlayground/

Look for these titles

Now Available

Jesse's Challenge
Mimosa Nights by Nicole Austin and TK Winters
Margarita Day by Nicole Austin and TK Winters

Recipe for a Mimosa Night: Take a few libations to loosen inhibitions, mix them with meddling college friends, add in an innocent game of dice, and the result is a steamy cocktail of erotic desires.

Mimosa Night
© 2006 Nicole Austin and TK Winters

Since her husband's military deployment, Reba has been plagued by dark, secret fantasies. Never before has she had such scandalously carnal needs—needs she can barely share with her husband, let alone anyone else. But her tenacious friends enlist the help of mysterious otherworld partners until she spills every spicy detail.

During an intimate reunion of college friends, three women share details of their own scorching real-life sexual experiences and the subsequent changes in their lives to help one friend find fulfillment. Things really start to sizzle, though, with an unexpected invitation, a mysterious delivery, and a once-in-a-lifetime offer Reba can't refuse.

From cowboys and porn stars to floggers and psi vamps, these ladies sure know how to unleash their fantasies.

Enjoy the following excerpt for *Mimosa Night:*

She heard the murmur of conversation before her eyes picked out the men standing in the cool shadows of the barn. Jase, arms crossed over his broad chest, leaned against the rough wood of a stall. Zeb's back rested on the hinged gate, one leg drawn up to brace the sole of his boot against the planks, muscular forearms draped across the top of the door. Katie felt as if all her senses went on high alert.

The musky, clean scent of cowboys mingled with the sweet hay lining the stalls was like an aphrodisiac racing through her bloodstream. Her womb clenched in response. There was an almost visceral feeling of testosterone rolling in heated waves from the two fine-looking cowboys to submerge her in desire.

As if aware of Katie on a deep, physical level, Jase turned toward her. He did nothing to hide his assessing gaze. Each place his gaze touched and lingered, her skin heated. When Zeb turned, letting his eyes roam over her sleek curves in silent perusal, the added intensity nearly melted her on the spot. All that masculine attention focused on her was somewhat disconcerting but oh-so-hot, causing her breath to catch, her heart to lodge in her throat.

Her nipples pebbled and she prayed her soft, button-down shirt was loose enough the men wouldn't notice her reaction. There was no way to hide the musky scent of her arousal, though, she thought with a shiver of excitement. She was certain they smelled her heated desire from where they stood.

Damn, she'd never gotten this sopping wet before, and in such record time. Her pussy lips swelled, thick cream coated her folds, soaking into her silky panties. Oh yeah, she was ready for some action.

As if reading her mind, Jase asked, "You finally ready, sugar?"

Katie whimpered as her womb clenched in response to his deep velvet voice stroking over her skin. The serious looks on their faces made it difficult to tell if they were teasing, or if their words meant what she prayed they did. Her body was ripe and prepared for them.

She'd imagined having an encounter with more than one man at a time, but it had always been just a fantasy—this had the potential of becoming real. Very real.

The idea held definite appeal when faced with these two gorgeous cowboys. They were such a study in contrasts, and she imagined their lovemaking styles would contrast as well. One demanding all she could give, but the other? She wasn't sure about Zeb. He seemed quiet and shy, but...but she absolutely had to find out, and this was it. If she wanted to live out her fantasy with these two men, now was the time to grab onto the opportunity with both hands and hold on for what was bound to be one wild ride.

Before she could untie her tongue, Zeb commented, "She sure looks ready, boss."

"Yes. I'm ready." Her voice was barely a whisper, but both men reacted to the husky, sensual sound by moving closer, crowding into her personal space. They both leaned in, their body language giving off a message rich with sexual desires Katie prayed she was reading correctly. Everything about them positively oozed sex.

She wanted them. Both of them. Right here. Right now. Vivid images of the two men pleasuring her at once had her breath coming in quick pants, her heart beating in a wild, discordant rhythm.

Zeb's hand rose, fingers brushing over her cheek. "You look a little flushed, baby." His soft blue eyes held both concern and desire.

Jase brushed his fingers over the row of buttons running from the waistband of her jeans to right above the swell of her breasts. "It's kinda warm in here, isn't it?" He teased the bare skin accessible through the opening, fingers gliding upward to linger over her rapidly beating pulse. "Maybe you should take some of these clothes off."

All the soft shyness left Zeb as he pressed in close against her right side. The hard, heated ridge of his erection caressed her hip and Katie felt sure she'd go up in flames. When the steely length of Jase's desire settled into the curve of her opposite hip, she began to tremble with anticipation.

These cowboys were big and hard all over. Yeehaw!

The two men continued moving forward, backing her up until she was held captive between the stall door and a wall of warm muscle. Each man gently grasped a slender arm, then large hands drew her arms to the side and forced her shoulders tight against the rough wood. With practiced ease, two cowboy boots—one scarred black, the other scuffed brown—pushed between her feet, easing her legs apart. The move forced her back to arch and her breasts to press forward.

Jase's warm hands slid down her body, stopping to cup and weigh one heavy breast, thumb rasping over her pebbled nipple.

At the same time, Zeb swooped in, his lips capturing hers. His hot, demanding mouth swallowed the sound of her gasp. His moist tongue teased at the seam of her lips until she opened for him and accepted a deeper mating of their mouths. Tongues twining and teasing, she took in his spicy, masculine flavor, imbibing the heady sensations. His free hand came up, fingers interlaced in her hair, tilting her head to the angle he desired. Once assured she would hold the position, he moved his hand to cup her other breast.

Both full globes felt needy and heavy as the men stroked and tugged her nipples through the soft and light material. Breaking the kiss, Zeb traced a path of fire over her jaw and down her neck. Katie let her head fall back and hang over the top of the stall door. The multiple sensations were powerful and overwhelming. All she could do was give herself over to their expert ministrations.

The front clasp of her bra was unhooked before Katie even realized her shirt had been unbuttoned. She moaned, reveling in the pressure of their warm hands teasing her flesh. She arched her back even more, filling their hands with the generous globes, seeking a firmer touch. A touch her cowboys were more than willing to provide.

Zeb's tongue plunged back within the hot, moist depths of her mouth, erasing any lingering questions in Katie's mind about how he would take her. His tongue moved in a seductive motion, a beautiful dance of give and take.

Jase's lips went to one aching breast. The first warm swipe of his tongue over the taut peak had her womb clenching and she moaned deeply. The vibrations raced through Zeb's mouth and his tongue began to thrust with even more intensity. Leaving her mouth once again, he teased the other nipple with lips, teeth and tongue.

Oh God, having both nipples suckled and teased at the same time was more erotic than anything she'd ever imagined.

Katie's legs shook from the extraordinary sensations her lovers created. She wouldn't be able to stand for much longer. Her knees weakened and threatened to buckle. She pictured herself sliding down the rough wood, a pool of boiling desire soaking into the hay, but Jase released her breast to slip one muscular thigh between her spread legs, forcing her onto her toes. Releasing his hold on her arm, Zeb palmed both aching breasts, teeth nipping, tongue swirling, fingers tweaking and pulling at the ultra-sensitive nubs.

Jase swirled his tongue across the delicate shell of her ear. He grasped the tender lobe between his teeth, the firm bite sending shivers racing down her spine. In a voice raspy with need, he commanded, "Ride my leg, sugar." He ground the hard length of his cock against her hip while moving his massive thigh, forcing Katie's jeans to rub against her trapped and aching clit. She couldn't think, couldn't breathe—the experience was too powerful and all-consuming.

"Jase...Zeb..."

"Ride me, Katie. Show me what a hot little filly you are," Jase demanded.

Zeb tugged hard on one elongated nipple while sucking the other swollen bud deep into his warm mouth. Hot jolts rocketed straight down to Katie's throbbing pussy, causing her hips to roll and grind harder against Jase's leg. She couldn't believe this was actually happening—her fantasy was coming to life.

Zeb released her breast with a wet pop and stood back to watch.

"Mmmmm...baby, you look so damn hot." One hand continued to grasp her breast and tease her nipple, while the other released the snap on her jeans and eased the zipper down. Slowly, Zeb worked his hand inside her jeans until his calloused palm rested above her mound, fingers cupping her swollen lips. Shifting his body slightly behind hers, he ground his hard shaft against her ass, thick fingers spreading her slick folds, and forcing her swollen clit to slide across the hard muscles of Jase's thigh.

"Oh. My. God." Katie's head rested against Zeb's broad shoulder as his arm snaked around her side, his other hand once again fondling her breast. Her back arched, bared breasts thrust forward, one nipple poking between Zeb's spread fingers, the other quivering and exposed.

Jase's heated breath flowed across her quivering flesh. "Damn, sugar. You are one beautiful sight." His mouth came down and pulled the exposed nipple deep inside his hot mouth, hands bracketing her hips to set the pace of her fevered motion.

Katie's hips bucked against Jase's leg as Zeb thrust against her from behind. Heat built and prickling sensations rushed across her skin. Little gasps and pants poured from between her kiss-swollen lips.

"Oh yeah," Zeb moaned. "Come for us now, Katie-girl."